DATE DUE		

September

September
a novel

Bridget Marks

Volt Press
Chicago and Los Angeles

08   07   06   05   04   5   4   3   2   1

Library of Congress Cataloging-in-Publication Data

Marks, Bridget.
September : a novel / Bridget Marks.
p. cm.
ISBN 1-56625-228-8

1. September 11 Terrorist Attacks, 2001—Fiction. 2. Terrorist victims' families—
Fiction. 3. Fugitives from justice—Fiction. 4. Intelligence officers—Fiction.
5. New York (N.Y.)—Fiction. 6. Socialites—Fiction. 7. Terrorists—Fiction. I. Title.

PS3613.A7545S47 2004
813' .6—dc22   2004009997

Volt Press
A division of Bonus Books
875 North Michigan Avenue
Suite 1416
Chicago, Illinois 60611

Printed in the United States of America

For Amber and Scarlett

Chapter One

IT WAS PRIMARY DAY IN THE NEW YORK CITY MAYORAL race. "The City that Never Sleeps" was bustling even earlier than normal on this beautiful September eleventh morning. Because of the term limit law he had been instrumental in passing, the current mayor, Rudy Giuliani, a Republican, would not be running for office. There would be a new mayor and he would most likely be a Democrat. So far, the hotly contested Democratic primary race seemed to be leaning toward one candidate in particular, Public Advocate Mark Green. This was just what gorgeous socialite Marielle Bennett had been hoping for. Green, her friend for thirty-five years, was a progressive like herself and would lead the city toward a new stability with a place at the table for all New Yorkers. She had known him from before the old Nader Raider days. If he won the primary he was a shoo-in and everybody knew it.

Marielle was a legend throughout political circles. As equally comfortable with right-wing conservatives as she was with left-wing radicals, she was loved and adored by everyone, revered not just for her amazing ability to "pick the pockets of the super rich," the phrase she used affectionately for fundraising, but even more for her dedication to the cause of civil rights. It was with the left wing that she truly identified. She had ridden the buses of the 1960s with activists like Angela Davis and Malcolm X. When Marielle would step off the bus at a rally, the fire hoses would literally be laid down, so commanding was her presence. She and Mark became instant compatriots. Over the years they worked side by side to see that the dreams of the 1960s were not lost to greed, avarice, and special-interest, goal-oriented politics.

Marielle was not the kind of supporter who just wrote a check and went home; and she didn't simply crawl into the trenches on the activists' coat tails. She inspired them and on this important September morning, while the other major Green supporters were just waking and starting their everyday lives, looking forward to attending what they hoped would be a victory party later that night, Marielle was up before dawn making sure she would be ready to open the polls at 6 AM at the Twenty-third Street Center for the Blind.

Marielle enjoyed being surrounded by the familiar friendly little group of die-hard politicos who never missed the chance to be part of a New York election. She was happy to see Tom McGinty, the burly Irish cop in charge of the voting machines. Tom had always been captivated by Marielle. Still stunning at fifty-eight years old, she looked like a forty-something version of 1950s superstar Grace Kelly. Tom used every excuse to engage her in conversation. When Marielle said she was thirsty, he ran across the street to get her a tea with cream, and a black coffee for himself—a big no-no, since a police officer had to be in attendance at all times for voting to be valid.

As the morning progressed, voters came and went. Suddenly the room began to buzz about an accident downtown at the World Trade Center.

"Did I hear you say that an airplane hit the World Trade Center?"

Marielle asked a tall well-dressed man in front of one of the voting booths.

"Yes it just happened," he answered. "A plane hit the North Tower, I heard about it on the radio in the taxi just as I was getting out. Probably just some crazy pilot or something. Don't worry, those towers aren't going anywhere. At the time they were built they were designed to withstand a plane strike."

Marielle did not hear anything after the word "yes." She could not believe a plane hit the World Trade Center. It was not possible. Fear began to overcome her.

"Oh my God, my son works there," she said as she fumbled in her purse for her cell phone. She dialed the phone and sighed with relief when she heard his voice on the other end of the line.

"Hi, Mom. Yes, we've been hit but the police and fire department have advised us to stay put," he reassured her. "It's very smoky but everything seems to be under control. Don't worry, I'll see you later and join you all for dinner. Let me go, I have to handle things here."

"We'll be at the Sheraton, honey, for Mark's victory party. I'm on the list with two guests. Just mention my name when you get up to Mark's suite."

"That's great. See you later Mom. Gotta get going. Love you."

"John Paul," she said. But he had already hung up.

"Whew," she said "Everything's okay."

"Of course it's okay, Mrs. Bennett. Just relax," Tom said, smiling. "Everything will be fine. Accidents do happen. As a young man my father worked in the Empire State Building. He was there that day during the war when the B-26 Liberation Bomber hit it. He talked about it till the day he died. It hit the 34th Street side at the 78th floor and the impact rocked the entire building. But the building is still there."

Voting continued for a while and then Tom's radiophone rang.

Marielle, who was still nervous about the situation, saw his face go ashen.

"Mrs. Bennett, I have to ask you and all other volunteers to begin evacuating the building. Voting is suspended. Just a few minutes ago a second plane flew into the other tower of the World Trade Center. They don't know for certain but they think it might be some kind of terrorist attack."

"How can that be?" she gasped in disbelief.

"Please, everyone must get out of here right now," he insisted. His phone rang again. "I've got to report downtown for duty immediately," he said hurriedly.

"Wait, Tom, I just can't believe this is happening," she cried. "Please, you have to take me with you. I'm worried about my son, John Paul. He will need me. I've got to get there and make sure he's all right."

"I don't think that's a good idea, Mrs. Bennett. Apparently it's chaos downtown right now and it's out of the question to take you."

"Look, Tom, I'm not trying to name drop here but I am a close friend of the mayor's. You know that. I need to go and I won't take no for an answer." She was almost hysterical now but firmly stood her ground. In an emergency like this the mayor probably wouldn't have the time to speak with even his closest friends. However she hoped Tom would fall for the bluff.

Tom, slightly in shock himself, grudgingly agreed. After clearing everyone out of the center, they dashed out of the building together. The squad driver who waited outside to rush Tom to the site was not thrilled at the prospect of having a civilian passenger. "No way is she coming, it's not protocol," the driver said. Tom opened the door for Marielle.

"Get in," he said looking at his fellow officer. "Don't even go there," he ordered. "Just drive."

As they navigated the traffic across 23rd Street to the West Side

Highway, Marielle tried to call her son back to assess the situation. Her mind was spinning. She heard Tom McGinty's words, *"terrorist attack,"* repeat in her mind. She began to feel a sickening fear. Then she heard her son's voice, "John Paul Bennett here ..." but before the automatic message could finish the phone went dead.

"At 10:05 AM this morning the South Tower of the World Trade Center collapsed." Everyone in the car became completely silent as the words came out of the radio. Fear came over Marielle in waves and she remembered another time in her life when she felt fear like this. Another September long ago. Another man, another place, another life.

As they drove down the West Side Highway toward the remaining tower of the Trade Center, smoke was billowing into the sky and the smell of burning was in the air. The radio was blaring and the words from headquarters describing the situation downtown were shockingly graphic. In trying to escape the fireballs within the building, victims were jumping out of the towers, falling like wounded birds to the pavement below. Marielle became dizzy and nauseated listening as she watched in horror while the second tower began to shake. "It's falling," she screamed.

A blinding dust cloud enveloped the windshield of the cruiser and it skidded to a halt, hitting a divider on the highway. Debris was falling everywhere. A huge steel girder hit the patrol car, smashing the windshield. The ground shook all around them.

Marielle could hear the officers coughing but couldn't see them very well. The car was filled with dust. The ground stopped vibrating and there was an eerie gray stillness.

"Tom, are you all right?" she asked.

She was worried about their safety. She knew Tom must be angry for letting her convince him to bring her along. She realized it had been a bad idea. As she sat there she felt something warm dripping into her eye.

She wiped at her eye. "Ouch," she said wincing. "I'm bleeding."

Luckily, both officers were unharmed. Tom helped Marielle out of the car and across the highway toward a dock by the Hudson River. Getting across to safe ground took some doing. There were broken pieces of building everywhere. It was as if the gates of hell had opened up and sent its demons to torment the earth. Tom noticed a piece of glass lodged in her forehead and removed it with his handkerchief.

"Press this hard," he said as he held the handkerchief to her forehead. "It looks like you may need stitches, Mrs. Bennett. Try to get back uptown and over to St. Vincent's Hospital. I'd take you there myself but I need to report for duty right now."

"No," she said. "I must know where my son is, how he is. I'll stay here by the river until you come back."

Marielle knew Tom had no time to argue with her. She also knew that he would not be able to come back for her. He was needed elsewhere. She would have to fend for herself. He squeezed her hand.

"Don't worry, I'll try to send help."

Marielle wanted to scream but could make no sound. John Paul could be one of those people who jumped from the building. He could have been in the falling tower. Hopefully he was able to get out. The uncertainty was paralyzing. "Dear God, who could have done this devil's act?" she thought.

The sound of fire engine and ambulance sirens drowned out all else. Marielle wanted to stop them from driving down the roadway; she wanted to jump onboard and try to find her son but she could only watch as they drove by. Such carnage in New York City was too much to imagine let alone live through. She started to laugh, and then cry, for in the midst of all this she had somehow hung on to her alligator Birkin bag—so tightly that the clasp cut into her hand. She took out her rosary and began to pray. Only yesterday she had been very upset over the fact that Madame Paulette's Dry Cleaners couldn't remove a stain from one of her favorite Chanel suits. It seemed really important at the time. And now things like that were so meaningless. "How life can change your perspective in an instant," she thought. Now the stains were not on a stupid suit, they were on her heart. Why? She kept asking God. Why? Why would He allow something so barbaric to happen?

Her head throbbed. She could see the fire although not clearly. There was so much black smoke where the majestic towers had been. It seemed only moments ago, then, she realized she was covered in gray dust.

"Save my son," she beseeched the rosary beads. She felt weak, her strength totally spent. She fell onto the dock, her legs no longer able to support her.

Tom McGinty made it to the site where the towers once stood. Mayor Giuliani had already arrived and had almost been killed himself. Tom didn't know him well and was aware of how preoccupied he was, but under the circumstances he felt obligated to tell him about Mrs. Bennett and the fact that he had left her on her own. The mayor actually cracked a smile. He understood very well how hard it was to say no to the lovely and persuasive Mrs. Bennett. He knew Tom McGinty was no match for the combination of her charm and determination. Hell, most politicians danced to the tune her money played, and she was always on the side of good and God to boot. He was concerned to hear she had been hurt, but he was more worried about her son.

It was well past noon before anyone came to help her, which seemed like an eternity. Marielle was in and out of consciousness from what would later be diagnosed as a severe concussion.

As Marielle lay on the dock, her eyes closed and her mind drifted to another September day long ago. It was 1969 and a tall man almost knocked her over in front of Saks Fifth Avenue. He had jumped out of a long black limousine with diplomatic plates that was literally blocking traffic on Fifth Avenue, much to the chagrin of a nearby police officer. In those days diplomatic plates meant you could drive and park anywhere no matter what or who you blocked.

She was amused by the whole thing as she watched this handsome James Bond–like figure of a man whose strong arms suddenly caught her as she nearly hit the pavement. With the wind almost knocked out of her, and desperately trying to catch her breath, Marielle found herself looking into the eyes of the most handsome man she'd ever seen.

His thickly lashed chocolate brown eyes danced, as he seemed to look right through her. His features were of the kind Michelangelo chiseled. Her stomach did that little jump you feel as a roller coaster descends.

"God, get hold of yourself," she thought as he helped her to her feet and guided her over to the curb. He had the softest skin she ever felt and his extraordinarily large hands were at the same time rugged yet gentle.

Although it was seconds, their eyes spoke a lifetime of hidden thoughts and dreams. It was almost as if they were kindred souls who might have shared other moments somewhere in another life.

"Madame, I'm terribly sorry. Are you all right? Did I hurt you?" he inquired, concerned.

Marielle was speechless. She tried to gather herself. The deep tone of his voice soothed her.

"You look very shaken. You can sit in my car and catch your breath. Better yet, my driver will take you wherever you wish to go."

"No, no, I'm fine," she murmured, embarrassed, straightening out her jacket.

As she turned to leave he took hold of her arm and said, "Wait, please. I'd appreciate it very much if you would call me." He handed her his card. She held it and stared at it, suddenly flustered. It read,

Ghani Irabi, Military Attaché to the Permanent Mission of Pakistan to the United Nations.

"I'm very flattered, but I'm married," she said almost biting her tongue as the words came out. She thought how foolish and childish she sounded considering she was a sophisticated, well-educated woman of the world.

He smiled that melt-your-heart kind of smile and replied, "So am I. Now promise you'll call." She hesitated. "Promise me," he said again not releasing her arm and holding her in his direct gaze. She looked away blushing.

She promised. She couldn't help herself. She felt drawn to this stranger; so handsome, so exciting. How naïve she had been. How could she have known the extraordinary events to come and how this day would change her life forever?

The smell of smoke and burning debris brought Marielle back into the present. She tried again to call John Paul. But now she heard nothing, only static. She opened her eyes a bit wider. Everything she saw was double. Her hands were covered in dried blood and her head was throbbing. She took a deep breath and again began to remember the past.

It was the spring of 1969. Marielle and her husband, Dr. Mortimer Bennett IV, had just moved into an estate in Oyster Bay Cove, "the Crest" it was called. Her mother, Elizabeth, had moved in with them to help raise their baby girl, Caroline, who was four years old.

The estate was beautiful; a dream come true. The majestic colonial sat at the top of a hill like a grande dame of the old Gold Coast mansions that dotted the North Shore of Long Island. It had seven bedrooms and four bathrooms and a separate servants' wing that Marielle had turned into a combination office space, playroom, and private quarters for her mother.

The gardens were reminiscent of the English countryside, and there was a blue stone path that led to the stables out back at the bottom of the hill.

Marielle's pedigree read like a Who's Who of American aristocracy. As a child she had everything anyone could ask for. Her presentation to society had been one of the most important and extravagant ever. Her social calendar was always full of the usual charity balls, horse shows, and society photo shoots.

Her husband, Morty, was sixteen years her senior, a world-famous scientist who spent most of his time in Washington. He had also been an advisor to President John F. Kennedy. He enjoyed the highest security clearance, called Q Crypto, and though some people thought he was a bit of a pompous ass, she always felt safe and protected around him. It was not a perfect marriage. Sometimes Marielle felt Morty was completely oblivious to her and her life. She was sure he enjoyed the performance of her wifely duties, but otherwise he mostly made her feel simple and even a tad boring when she was around him.

Marielle accepted her husband's distant personality. He had been her first and only lover. She had nothing and no one to compare him with. Her mother and father had been somewhat reserved as well, so his cool, removed attitude was exactly what she was used to and it seemed normal to her. Their marriage, though uninspired, had been happy in a quiet and proper sort of way.

Morty was a child prodigy. He skipped numerous grades and ended up the youngest graduate ever from Harvard and MIT. He told Marielle he seldom dated as a young man and was subsequently very shy around the opposite sex. Morty blamed his overbearing mother who didn't trust women, and until she died when he was thirty-five, he told Marielle, she came between him and every woman he tried to date.

He also told her that everything in his life changed for the better when he came to Smith College as part of Senator Ted Kennedy's lecture group. She remembered they had instantly hit it off and since the group was spending the weekend in Hyannisport, the senator, sensing how much Morty liked her, took it upon himself to invite Marielle to join them.

"Of course, you'll stay in Mother's house," the senator reassured her.

"I would love to go," she said.

She fit in quite naturally with the Kennedy insiders. She knew the family found her a delight, especially when she played on the winning touch football team. They loved horsing around and she was an eager participant in their active lifestyle. Morty eagerly watched her play from the sidelines for hours and then told her how fascinated he was that a girl could be so interested in his work. She allowed him to bend her ear all through dinner and well into the night. She was hungry for knowledge and they spent a lot of time exchanging ideas but mostly Marielle just listened.

They also discovered they shared a huge passion for riding and fox hunting. Marielle came from a family of avid horsewomen. Her mother was "whipper-in" for the Essex Hunt and did a good job keeping the hounds in line. Marielle invited Morty to come spend the weekend with her family and cap with the hunt. Riding was a sport he truly enjoyed and it was one of the few activities his mother had approved of as an outlet for her otherwise bookish son. Essex was one of the few remaining hunts for live fox. Most hunts were now drag hunts where the scent of the fox was literally dragged by horsemen over the terrain.

Marielle could tell how wonderful Morty felt when they were together. She sensed how pleased he was to be in the role of the powerful older man. Marielle was young and full of life; her spirit was infectious. Morty would later tell her that their courtship was the happiest time of his life. He had found his princess and all the pieces of his world suddenly began to fit perfectly together. They had a storybook wedding and honeymoon in St. Maarten at his family's villa. And then a few years later Caroline came along. In Morty's mind, he had his own Camelot and for him life was perfect.

Unfortunately, Marielle didn't know how to communicate and felt lonely and unhappy a good deal of the time. She didn't know how to tell him that he didn't satisfy her in the way she needed. No one had ever educated him as to the art of pleasing a woman and Marielle had only known him. She did love her husband and enjoyed his touch and their lovemaking but she always knew something was missing. She just didn't know what—until that September day with Ghani. She realized that Morty's touch did not give her goose bumps the way the dark stranger's did.

Still, she was always trying to impress Morty, and on that fateful September day she couldn't wait to tell the good doctor about her little adventure in front of Saks.

As they sat down to dinner in their huge dining room that evening in 1969, she moved from her place at the end of the table to sit alongside him. His displeasure at her informal behavior was dispelled as she began gushing about her "day."

"Oh Morty, you'll never believe what happened to me," she said as she proudly waved Mr. Irabi's card like a trophy she had won.

Morty was amused in spite of himself as he perused the card. "How nice, my dear," he said. "So you met some high-ranking Pakistani diplomat. Who knows where that could lead? Jackie Kennedy got an exceptional horse from General Zia a few years ago. You know, the one she boards out at Fox Chase. Sardar, I think she calls it. Maybe the embassy will give you a nice horse, too."

He was being sarcastic and she knew it. Morty always had a way of teasing her and making light of anything she did. She tried not to let it bother her, but as they made love that night her thoughts were on the handsome stranger. When it was over Morty asked her as he always did, "Did I make you feel as good as I did?"

"Yes, darling, of course you did," she said, wondering why he felt the need to ask this question.

"I'm going downstairs to get your ice cream, would you like some cookies and milk with it?" he said.

She smiled. He always got her ice cream after they made love like some sort of reward for good behavior. It had started on their wedding night and continued until it was almost a tradition. *Thank God it only happens once a week or I'd be a two-ton Tess,* she mused. Morty was so cute she forgave him for being so predictable.

She went into the bathroom and wet a washcloth with hot water. As she cleaned herself off in front of the mirror she wondered if Ghani Irabi would find her body attractive. She looked critically at herself. Her breasts never were the same after she'd nursed Caroline. They just didn't stand up the way they used to. She began to fantasize about how it would feel if Ghani were to caress her breasts. She pictured his face so close to hers, she could still smell his hot sweet breath on her. She felt excited.

"Honey, come get your ice cream," Morty called.

Abruptly the mood was broken and she instantly felt guilty. "Coming, just a minute," she said composing herself. She hoped he would just go to sleep. She wanted to be alone. She didn't feel like a science lecture. She just wanted to eat her ice cream in peace.

However, Morty had the oil crisis he perceived was coming on his mind and began to expound.

"Those Capitol Hill idiots couldn't see the forest for the trees if their lives depended on it. They're going to have a real problem on their hands if they don't listen to me. Prices could double and, hell it's a finite resource. They've got to start developing alternate renewable energy sources. Solar or wind power aren't the enemy, for crying out loud, they are the technologies of the future."

He went on and on until Marielle yawned and said, "Darling it's almost 2 AM."

"I'm sorry, honey. I always do this to you. I get so frustrated with these shortsighted boobs. There's just no cure for stupidity, you know." He got up out of bed and picked up the empty ice cream bowl on the nightstand. "I've got some ideas I want to jot down. See you in the morning, sweetheart."

Marielle shook her head, propped up her pillows and turned out the light. As she drifted off to sleep she hoped her dashing new friend was thinking of her, too.

As soon as she was alone the following morning Marielle called the Pakistani Mission to the United Nations. "Good morning," she said. "May I speak with Mr. Ghani Irabi's office?"

"This is Mr. Irabi's office," the secretary said. "May I be of help?"

"This is Marielle Bennett; Mr. Irabi asked me to call today."

"Oh yes, Madame. Mr. Irabi said he was expecting your call. However he is in a meeting right now. Please give me your address as he wants to messenger an invitation to you and your husband for a dinner party this weekend at our mission honoring the Soviet ambassador."

At the party that Saturday night they were announced as they entered the ballroom. "Doctor and Mrs. Mortimer Bennett IV." All eyes were on her, ambassadors and businessmen, watching her every move.

Suddenly a sharp pain went through her head and she found herself back in the present. She heard a paramedic say, "I think she's with us. Ma'am, Ma'am can you hear me? You're going to be all right. We're taking you to the hospital. Don't be afraid; we're here to help. Do you have any allergies?"

"No," she replied weakly. "My son, John Paul Bennett who works for Morgan Stanley, was in the North Tower. Can you find out if he's all right?"

"What floor was his office on, Ma'am?"

"82, 84." She couldn't think straight. "His cell number is 917-555-4700. I've tried but can only get static."

"All cell phones are out, Ma'am, because of the loss of the satellite on top of the towers."

As the ambulance pulled into triage at St. Vincent's Hospital she tried to sit up. The paramedics wouldn't let her. She felt helpless, and demanded to speak to whomever was in charge.

The press was everywhere. One of the reporters heard a paramedic say he had a VIP in need of admission. "Marielle Bennett's in that ambulance," he said, scrambling. "It's unclear if she was in one of the towers or what. Let's get a statement from her."

In a moment, the vultures—as she liked to call them—were trying to take her picture and shoving their microphones in her face. Security intervened and they carried her into the ER on a stretcher.

Her only thoughts were of her son.

"I'm Dr. Osgood," a smiling young man said as he took her hand. "Looks as if you've had quite a blow to the head. A pretty bad concussion, but as far as I can see, with a little rest you'll be as good as new. I'll get a plastic surgeon to come stitch you up. We have to keep that beautiful face beautiful, don't we?"

"I don't care about me; just my son," she said.

"We have contacted your daughter and she's on her way. You try to rest now. I hope your son will be found soon," he said reassuringly. He started to leave.

"Please, Doctor, wait. Where are the survivors being taken? Maybe someone knows if my son is all right and if he's been taken to a hospital."

"There don't seem to be too many survivors as yet," he stated plainly. "Perhaps once the debris is cleared and they can get in there they'll find people alive. I understand how you must be feeling. It's just so hard to get your mind around this. This kind of thing doesn't happen here. We are so unprepared for it." He shook his head.

"How could anyone be prepared for something so senseless?" Suddenly she thought how meaningless her wealth and position really were. She was just another mother driven to the point of anguish over her child.

After her stitches were completed, her daughter Caroline arrived. "Oh Mummy, it's pandemonium out there. Are you all right?" she asked catching her breath and giving her mother a gentle hug.

"Why are you so winded Caroline?" Marielle asked.

"You have no idea, Mummy. The city is at a standstill. There were no cabs. So I went to my garage and then I couldn't even get the car out because the attendant wasn't there. I walked forty blocks and thank God you're okay."

"Have you heard anything about your brother?" Marielle asked worriedly.

"No Mummy, but I'm sure he got out."

Marielle wasn't convinced at all.

"I've arranged to move you up to Lenox Hill." Caroline continued. "After all, wouldn't it be better to be in the care of people we know?"

"Dr. Osgood has been wonderful to me," Marielle replied.

"Oh Mother, this could be serious. A concussion is nothing to fool around with."

At that moment, Dr. Osgood came into the room.

"The head nurse just informed me you're thinking about moving to Lenox Hill. Frankly bouncing around in an ambulance in your condition is not what I recommend Mrs. Bennett. Perhaps in a day or so . . . "

Caroline cut him off. "I'm Lady Caroline Harlington, Mrs. Bennett's daughter. Dr. Vincent Lancelotti, head of neurosurgery, is a family friend and has made the arrangements," she said looking directly at his ear as she spoke to him.

Marielle was familiar with this method of disrespect. She'd learned it at finishing school herself. This was how high-born ladies were taught to deal with people who were clearly beneath them. She hated seeing Caroline employ it. Marielle knew St. Vincent's was a little too common for her. Caroline had become so snooty since she married Patrick. She's nothing like me. She couldn't care less about Dr. Osgood's feelings or anyone else's. She knew her daughter's opinion of her work with the less fortunate and it upset her at a time like this to have her act like this.

Marielle was close to hysteria now. No word about John Paul, and Caroline upsetting the doctors and nurses with her usual superior attitude. The orderlies from the private ambulance company had arrived. She was on her way to Lenox Hill. As Caroline said, "Wouldn't it be better to be in the care of people we know?" Marielle desperately needed to know something—anything—about John Paul.

Caroline accompanied her in the ambulance. After more than a few attempts Caroline reached the mayor's private number on her cell phone. "Rudy, it's me, Caroline Larson. Mom's not seriously injured but she's just hysterical about John Paul. Do you think there's any hope for my brother?" she asked.

"Of course there's hope," Rudy assured her, despite what he feared. The mayor never gave up hope, not for the friends he knew who were in the towers or for the police and firemen. He would hope and carry on the rescue long after all others gave up, "Caroline, pray for your brother and everyone else. Pray hard. It's all we can do right now. And tell your mother I'm thinking about her and will let her know the minute I get any word about John Paul."

Chapter Two

MARIELLE ARRIVED AT LENOX HILL HOSPITAL AND was whisked to the private room that had been prepared for her. The room looked more like a hotel suite than a hospital room. Caroline had made sure her favorite flowers, lilies of the valley, were on the night table beside her bed. She had also had brought over a picture of herself and John Paul taken last summer at the family's summer home in East Hampton.

What a contrast they were; she blond and blue eyed, John Paul so dark, his coal-black hair and eyes and fabulous smile peering out of the photograph. How tongues had wagged over the years about how different they looked. It was hard to believe they were brother and sister. After the death of her father two years ago, Caroline asked her mother if there had ever been anyone else in her life, but Marielle assured her, "There's never been anyone but Daddy. John Paul's just a throwback to the black Irish in us, like your Grandma Elizabeth used to say."

As they wheeled Marielle into the room, Caroline felt relief. *Thank God she's here and safe,* she thought.

Marielle was immediately tended to by Dr. Vincent Lancelotti. He was very close to the Bennetts and had flown his entire family to

England to attend the wedding when Caroline married Lord Harlington. He concurred with Dr. Osgood's diagnosis. He was pleased with the look of her stitches and reassured Caroline that her mother would be just fine. He was going to order an MRI just to be on the safe side, but he was confident there was nothing to worry about.

Marielle tried to relax, but the MRI at Lenox Hill was an enclosed unit and it didn't help that she was slightly claustrophobic. She was no longer in shock and already had an MRI performed at St. Vincent's so it annoyed her to have to do it again. The noisy clanging as the machine did its work made the unpleasantness even worse. *Does Dr. Lancelotti really believe that St. Vincent's MRI isn't as good because it's a lesser hospital?* she asked herself. The whole idea of that made her angry. She disliked snobbery in any form.

Marielle tried to get her thoughts off the present. Soon she was back at the Pakistani mission and all the glory of that other September night long ago. Russian Ambassador Malik was the guest of honor. He was well versed in Dr. Bennett's research work and the two of them hit it off very well. Ambassador Malik, Dr. Bennett, and Soviet Science Attaché Yuri Nemkov spent most of the evening discussing some of the new technologies Dr. Bennett had been working on. Marielle knew we were in the middle of the Cold War but scientists paid no attention to such political details. They seemed especially interested in his breakthrough solar laser technology which could deliver 3 trillion joules of energy per second. "In theory it's a clean kill weapon." Morty explained, "It makes a hydrogen bomb look like a walk in the park. A strategic weapon with no fallout, only an instant vaporization of the target."

The two diplomats listened intently as he continued. "This could be useful against an incoming missile or even an asteroid coming from deep space. My hope is that it could be controlled by the United Nations for civilian purposes to protect the entire world, not just by one country for military domination," he concluded.

Marielle had heard Morty explain his work innumerable times. In fact, he often used her as a sounding board for his new inventions. He enjoyed taking her step by step through every detail so she would understand the patents, which the family owned. "Just in case the day comes when I'm not here," he'd tell her.

Rather than standing there listening to the three men talk, occasionally prompting Morty if he missed a word, Marielle politely excused herself and began to meander through the distinguished crowd. She made her way to the sumptuous buffet line. Miriam Hasan, the Pakistani deputy ambassador's wife, put her arm around her and said, "There is someone in my husband's office who wants very much to see you. Here, I'll fill your plate. You go over to where my husband is motioning to you."

Miriam's husband, Jamil Hasan, was a quiet man, although very nice looking. He asked her to follow him and led her along a narrow corridor to his private office where Ghani was waiting for her.

All of a sudden Marielle felt very nervous. She could feel her heart beating in her throat and her cheeks were hot. She had come here hoping to see him again, but expected them to meet among the crowd of guests. But now they would be alone and she was afraid of what might happen. She knew she'd probably make a fool of herself, so strong was her attraction to him.

For a moment she felt like turning around and running back to her husband, pretending to be ill, and going home. That sixth sense which tells you to run like hell should have been heeded; a fact she would come to understand much later.

Ghani at once was by her side looking at her with what can only be described as hungry eyes, the kind that seem to look directly into your soul.

"I am happy to see you again, please sit here," he said, taking her hand and leading her to a comfortable leather sofa. "If you are as beautiful on the inside as you appear to be on the outside, I feel you will do something that will make the world a better place." She was mesmerized and in awe. She never felt as she did that night, the night he kissed her for the first time. For the next hour he spoke to her of everything: poetry, children, religion, politics, his wives.

"Marielle, I have a secret to tell you about me. I don't know why I want to tell you, but I am a poet of sorts. Would you like to hear one I wrote about how we met?" he asked.

Marielle was touched. Writing a poem about her was the most romantic thing anyone had ever done for her.

She blushed. "Yes, Ghani, of course I'd like to hear it."

He recited almost shyly:

> *Just another day.*
> *Until the fates brought you my way.*
> *The sunshine in your hair.*
> *Your lovely face so fair.*
> *My heart began to pound.*
> *Could it be true love I've found?*
> *Or am I just a fool*
> *Would Allah be so cruel?*

He finished, smiling at her and looking deep into her eyes.

Marielle was bowled over. He was talking to her of love like he'd known her all his life and to her surprise she felt the same.

Ghani spoke of his childhood in the refugee camps. He described the terror as bombs rained down on them. "Israeli bombs," he said, "made in the USA." His mother had given him spoonfuls of honey to calm her little boy as the explosions came closer and closer to the little room in which they all lived. "Honey makes me think of those awful days," he told her.

Marielle tried to comfort him. *How terrible for children who endure war,* she thought. They are often scarred for life. "This must have been a difficult time in your life," she said.

"After my mother and father were killed, I felt lost. My brother and sister both died of malnutrition when I was very little, so I had no one. Then Allah smiled on me. One day a Saudi prince came to the camp to view the conditions there. He took pity on me and took me to live in Saudi Arabia with his family. I studied at an Islamic religious school in my youth, and later I was educated in England at Harrow and Oxford, as my benefactor ran many business interests from there. We became so close I married into his family. My first wife was barren so I married again, this time to a Pakistani girl who so far has only given birth to four girls. One day I long for a son."

"What a fascinating life you've led," she began, moving closer to him. Their eyes met and she lost her train of thought. Flustered, she couldn't finish her sentence. She was trying to think of something to say and started laughing but before she could speak he swept her into his arms and kissed her. She returned the kiss with a fire she never felt before or ever imagined.

She was filled with desire for him and wanted to continue passionately kissing him, but he pushed her back, murmuring, "There will be time for that, my dear. There is so much I long to share with you. The reason I have come to this country; my hopes for a free and prosperous Palestine. There is so much to do," he said. "Medicine to buy, schools to build, people to deliver services to, people to train and mold so that changes come. Hunger and poverty must become a thing of the past. The yoke of oppression by the Israelis must be lifted."

Marielle sat there like a child at the feet of a god figure, listening to his words, understanding his thoughts, feeling his emotions. She always wanted to matter in the scheme of things. She always wanted to do something important for the people who had so much less than she did. She longed to make a difference in the world. And now, for the first time, she was getting the feeling that maybe she could.

Jamil Hasan quietly knocked on the door and entered the room. "Ghani, Dr. Bennett is looking for his wife. I think he's noticed that she has been missing for a while. You two must be more discreet," he said smiling.

Marielle, embarrassed, quickly averted her eyes. At that moment Miriam entered the room and said, "You're in need of repair."

Marielle realized her lipstick must be all over her face and turned a deep crimson red.

"Don't worry my sweet American friend. We'll tell your husband you've been upstairs with me in the private quarters seeing my children, Ramiz and Rima."

Chapter Three

THE VALIUM DRIP HELPED MARIELLE SLEEP THROUGH most of the night of September 11th. She felt secure in the safety of the Lenox Hill Hospital, dreaming of her lost love. Morning dawned and the nurses woke her up as they entered her room with their blood pressure machines. At once she remembered what had happened the previous day and sat up in bed. "My son—do you have any news about my son?"

Maureen Reilly, the night-duty nurse, was about to go home. Her morning relief person had just come on. She had been looking in on Marielle all night, waiting for an opportunity to speak with her. Maureen loved to read the society pages of all the newspapers and was very familiar with the name Marielle Bennett. Although they had never met, she felt as though she knew her. Now finally they would talk. Maureen took Marielle's hand, "Do you have a photograph of him? I'll make copies of it and go downtown myself to get it to the proper agencies. I've got the rest of the day off. I'm a widow and I know how I'd feel if it were one of my boys. Thank God all three of them work on Long Island."

Marielle opened her purse and took out a snapshot of John Paul from her wallet, which she handed to Maureen. She was so grateful she didn't know what to say. Tears streamed down her face. She wanted to search for John Paul herself, but was physically unable.

The relief nurse came into the room. She went over to the chart and began reading. Her name was June Winters. Her Middle Eastern heritage was very evident in her appearance. She was not attractive in the sense that Maureen Reilly was, and she seemed self-conscious about it. The events of the day before had been very hard on her. Since the terrorist attacks were performed by radical Muslims, there was a backlash against anyone who appeared even remotely Middle Eastern. On her way to work she had been verbally attacked.

Realizing what Mrs. Bennett must be going through, June hoped she wouldn't upset her just by being there. June started to take her pulse when Dr. Lancelotti came into the room. He couldn't believe how small and helpless Marielle looked, her eyes swollen from the blow to her head as well as from her tears of worry for her son. Hoping to somehow console Marielle while being totally oblivious to June, he launched into a tirade.

"Those filthy Arab bastards. We'll get them. We should start deporting every Muslim son of a bitch we can get our hands on." He paused; collecting himself realizing this was the wrong tack. He took a deep breath. "I'm sorry. There is still no word on John Paul but the mayor himself has called twice this morning to see how you are doing."

Marielle, in spite of her grief, couldn't let the doctor speak in such a hateful way. "Vincent, whoever did this evil should be punished, but please don't think for a minute that all Muslim people are evil. They aren't. Timothy McVeigh was a monster. Surely you don't think all blue-eyed Irishmen are evil, too, because of him. The same is true of our Arab brothers and sisters. Few of them would wish such horror on the innocent."

June Winters took it all in, trying to be inconspicuous, wishing she could blend into the woodwork. June needed this job and

Dr. Lancelotti was acting like he wanted to tear a Muslim—any Muslim—limb from limb.

Marielle thought how much people are the same. In anger, they lash out at anyone they think is like whomever they perceive to be the enemy. "All humans have a little terrorist in their hearts if they allow their hatred to take over," she said trying to smooth June's ruffled feathers. Marielle sensed that June was relieved that someone had compassion for Muslims.

Dr. Lancelotti, embarrassed, told her he would look in on her later. "Overall you are doing well but your blood pressure is high. If it comes back to normal and there are no complications with your concussion, I might let you go home tomorrow morning." She thanked him for coming to see her and said she needed to be downtown until John Paul was found.

"Vincent, please pray for his safety. Do you think anyone can survive under all that steel and cement?"

"Many people will be found alive. God willing, John Paul will be among them." He didn't have the heart to tell her that so far no survivors had been found.

After Dr. Lancelotti left, June carefully changed the dressings on Marielle's bandages. "Your stitches have been perfectly done. There will most likely be no scarring. Is there was anything I can get for you, or do to make you more comfortable?"

"Yes, I'd really like to have a cup of hot tea with a little milk and maybe you'll sit down and talk to me. I need to talk to someone."

"I'll be right back."

June left to get the tea. When she returned Marielle was sobbing. June set the tea down and put her arm around her. "Don't give up hope. It will be all right," June said, patting her on the shoulder.

Marielle looked at her and was glad her nurse was Middle Eastern. "Just pray for my son," she said. "His name is John Paul."

"You're very lucky. I always wanted a son. But my husband was in the service here in the U.S. and it never happened. Perhaps that was for the best. We got a divorce ten years ago. I became a nurse and I love my work. Of course I will pray for your son. Try to rest now, dear, you need it. If you want to be discharged in the morning, you have to relax so the medication you've been given can lower your blood pressure. Close your eyes now; I'll be sitting right over here if you need me."

Marielle weakly reached out for June's hand. "Thank you," she said. "John needs someone to pray to Allah," she said sleepily. She knew that June would think it was strange for her to speak of Allah the way she did. But she didn't care. As she drifted into sleep June remarked that her son's eyes looked as if they belonged to someone who could only have come from the desert.

As the morning of September 12th slipped into afternoon, Marielle was unable to sleep very much. Her mind was tortured, as any mother's would be. The worst part was the uncertainty. She was determined to be released today. She kept her eyes closed, feigning sleep so the nurse would write a good report. Half awake, half asleep she could not escape the past, which, like a hard piece of asphalt was rising and hitting her with a load of memories.

Once again she remembered 1969. How honored she was to attend the party at the Pakistani mission. How excited she was in the company of her new friends. How impressed she was with Ghani. In order to try to unite her old world with her new one, she had given a party to introduce everyone to her social set. Ironically, it had actually been Morty's suggestion. He liked entertaining at home and thought their circle of close friends would enjoy meeting these diplomats and that it would provide him with the opportunity to show off their new home with its exquisite grounds and interior.

Her mother worked so hard on the decorations and details. Everything had to be perfect for her daughter's special night.

As the guests arrived Marielle became increasingly anxious for

Ghani to get there. How wonderful those first feelings of anticipation were as the whirlwind romance began to unfold. He was dazzling, she remembered. No woman could have resisted him. It was as if no one else was there that night as she showed him her new home. He laughed at her doll collection and the teddy bear on her bed.

"You really are a little girl at heart, sweet Marielle," she could still hear him say. She could still see his smile and feel his presence too, as if it were only yesterday.

She also felt her mother's searing look as they descended the staircase together.

"You have other guests, my dear," she admonished Marielle as she led Ghani away and out to see her greenhouse. Marielle always wondered if her mother knew even then how crazy she was about him.

Marielle was dazzled as Ghani drew her deeper and deeper into the intrigue that colored his life. He opened her eyes to so much she never knew. So much she never even dreamed of. He took her to closed sessions of the Security Council meetings within the United Nations. When the United States ambassador objected to her presence, Ghani flaunted his influence by having Soviet Ambassador Malik personally invite her as a guest of the USSR.

During one such closed session the Belgian government presented the most damning evidence ever seen on the injustices in Vietnam, particularly the incident at Mai Lai. It included U.S. military training films where young soldiers were shown women holding babies begging for help who were actually suicide bombers. Then it showed training sessions where our U.S. servicemen bayoneted dolls and shot dummy women and children with Asian features. Their commander was screaming, "Death to all gooks." This was followed by graphic war footage.

Marielle had a love for humanity and was horrified by this picture of the ugly American being presented to the world. When the Belgian Ambassador then demanded a statement from the United

States as to their position on their films and the battlefield atrocities, she was further disillusioned when the U.S. ambassador simply said, "No comment."

"Does no American have a comment?" the wily old diplomat chided his American counterpart. Again there was silence but this time Marielle rose from her seat in the Soviet box and said, "Mr. Chairman, I am Marielle Bennett, an American citizen, and I have a comment. For the first time in my life I am ashamed to be an American."

The entire room became so quiet a pin could be heard to drop. Ghani turned to Malik. "It's not every day one finds so lovely a woman who is so well suited to our purpose; a real natural. She will be useful to me in many ways."

"Ghani, be careful. From the way you look at her I think your own feelings may come back to bite you," he replied.

During a break, Ghani told her America was part of a Zionist plot to commit genocide on the poor and downtrodden of the world, including people of color, Palestinians and the Vietnamese.

"Didn't you see with your own eyes your young American soldiers committing unspeakable murderous acts on children, old people, unarmed people? I want to show you the truth. This is what your country is really doing," he said, earnestly taking her by the shoulders.

"Ghani, couldn't this have been an isolated incident?"

"No, Marielle, my darling, it is neither isolated nor one incident. Your country is committing genocide on the North Vietnamese people just as Israel does to my people. These powers have a hidden agenda. I'm sorry to be the one to point this out to you, but it's important to me for you to know."

Before she could even digest what he said they were ushered back into the chamber. As they entered he put his arm around her protectively, it felt so natural.

The council reconvened and began to deal with the alleged burial alive of a Palestinian girl by the Israeli army. Marielle was shocked when after irrefutable evidence was presented the council decided not to make the incident public because the anti-Jewish sentiment that would be stirred up could trigger an even greater conflict in the region. She turned to Ghani, shocked at what she'd heard. He gently squeezed her hand.

Ghani wanted to share the plight of his people, the Palestinians, with Marielle, and his desire for a homeland for them. He admired her blind love of humanity and her passion for providing all people with a decent human life. He skillfully fanned the flames of moral right and wrong in Marielle's kind heart. He wasn't sure himself of why he cared so much what she thought. For reasons he couldn't explain he trusted her, even though in the past he had trusted no one but himself.

As they ate lunch in the delegates' dining room he remarked that the tragic murder of the Palestinian girl was the rule rather than the exception in the Holy Land.

As a boy in the camps he had seen dozens of people tortured and killed by Israeli soldiers. The conditions he described were deplorable. There was no running water, not just for days, but for weeks; no doctors, no medicine. The International Red Cross was most often barred by the Israelis from helping them.

Marielle tried to understand how his suffering made him blame the problems of the world on what happened in an area the size of a postage stamp in the Middle East. "Ghani, you must forgive what happened to you. Anger and hate help no one. You must work for peace and understanding. The Israelis are like all people. There are good and bad. I am not denying there has been injustice. There is injustice everywhere, even here in our early Founding Fathers' treatment of the Native Americans. But we've gotten past trying to kill each other. We are trying to make life better by improving their opportunities for education and inclusion in mainstream American life."

"This can happen in the Middle East, too. Look at the example of Anwar Sadat and his wonderful wife. Darling, I know you can't forget your painful past, but you can forgive. It's only in forgiving that we can find true nobility and strength."

Ghani was deeply touched by the simple and sincere outlook she presented as a cure-all to things large and small. Like Fatima who served the Prophet Mohammed so well, she was pure of thought. He felt remorse for his plans to use her. He pushed aside these romantic notions although he knew he was falling in love with her, and in some ways her words were blinding him and making him question himself. He prayed to Allah for the courage to remain true to the holy Jihad he had dedicated himself to. But he also prayed to Allah for her. He asked Him to protect an infidel.

Ghani did not share his violent side with her; the means by which his people would achieve their goals. He indulged her goodness and belief in the teachings of Mahatma Gandhi. She told him, "Wishing death to any people, even one's oppressors, is evil in itself. Hatred must be returned with acceptance, violence with love, unfairness with forgiveness. You know, Ghani, I actually marched next to Martin Luther King, Jr. He was such a humble man, yet he was a giant as he proudly led the way to a better life for black citizens here in America. He emulated Mahatma Gandhi's peaceful yet firm protest of injustice. Your people should employ the same strong but non-violent resistance. It could work. I can promise you that violence never will resolve anything."

He held her face in his hands lovingly.

"Marielle, it's so cute that you think the problems of the world could be solved so easily but then that's what is so special about you my sweet angel," he said realizing how affected he was by her. "Shhh, I just want to kiss you. We can solve the ills of the world later." He laughed, sliding his hand under her skirt and gently brushing her thigh.

"Ghani, people will see us. Stop," she said, but she was as excited as he was. She felt a twinge of guilt but it quickly passed. He was a temptation and she felt powerless over it.

He was falling deeply in love with her and knew she would have been disappointed in him and repulsed by his need to see every Israeli man, woman, and child driven into the sea. He hid his dark ambitions to bask in the glow of his newly found love and sought to twist her perceptions to suit his own purposes.

Marielle began to see that what the public knew as truth was really lies created in those closed sessions by men with an agenda that had nothing to do with right and wrong. Her innocence was left on the altar of deception that is part and parcel of the United Nations. She was too naïve to realize how she was being used, or the repercussions her outburst would have on her husband and his government contracts.

Poor Morty wasn't ready for the tongue lashing he'd receive at the Pentagon over this. It didn't take long for word to spread that his wife was becoming an ardent sympathizer for the antiwar movement and that foreign nationals were using her to discredit her government.

Morty had been in Washington, D.C., working in his Pentagon office nearly around the clock for the past several days when he was called to a meeting in Colonel Haig's office. He assumed it was about their current project and brought with him his briefcase with his most recent notes. To his surprise and dismay, the meeting concerned his wife.

"What does Marielle's opinion on the Vietnam War have to do with the price of eggs?" he said, laughing.

"This is no joking matter," the colonel said seriously. "Yesterday, your wife publicly embarrassed this government in a closed session of the UN Security Council. Do you have any idea with whom she is keeping company?"

Morty scratched his head. "Well I know she's been quite friendly with the Pakistani ambassador's wife," he said, shrugging.

"We're not talking about wives, Dr. Bennett. We are talking about your wife sitting with the Soviet ambassador and verbally trashing her country. You get her under control," he ordered.

"Look," Morty said, "Marielle is a caring, compassionate woman. She views her country as the savior of the world. Can I help it that a lot of the stuff we're doing these days wouldn't play well in Sunday School class in Peoria? I'll do my best to put a lid on her friendship with these foreigners."

Colonel Haig knew Morty's work was essential to national security so he decided to let this ride. If no further problem came to light, it was in everyone's interest to forget about it.

Morty went back to his office a little shaken and perplexed. He picked up the phone to call Marielle but decided it was better to confront her in person. Despite the fact that he was supposed to stay in Washington for several more days, he decided he needed to get back to Oyster Bay immediately. On the train ride home all he could think of was what the hell she had done to upset the brass. He didn't really care about politics. All he knew was that he'd put a stop to whatever it was so he could get on with important things, mainly his scientific research. He didn't relish this impending confrontation. He was a man of logic not emotion. He and Marielle rarely fought, but whatever this was had gone too far. He'd see to it that she confined her activities to her charity work and nothing else.

He arrived home and was greeted by little Caroline who jumped into his arms. "Hi Daddy, I've missed you," she gushed.

"Me too. Let's go find Mummy," he said.

"Mummy's in the city," the precocious child quipped.

Morty was annoyed but didn't show it. "Run along sweetheart

and find your grandma. Daddy needs to do some work. Tell her I'll be in the den."

Morty made himself an unusually strong scotch and sat down in his favorite chair to smoke his pipe. As he looked at his watch, he wondered what the hell Marielle was still doing in the city at a quarter of seven at night.

Grandmother Elizabeth came into the den.

"Morty, what a surprise. We didn't expect you until the weekend. Marielle is in the city with Miriam Hasan. Did she know you were coming home tonight?" she asked.

"No," Morty said. "What time did she say she'd be back?"

"She won't be home; she's staying the night at the apartment. I thought you knew."

"No, she didn't mention it," he said, getting up. "That's all right, I'll just drive in and see her there."

"Is anything wrong?" Elizabeth inquired. "You seem on edge."

Morty didn't answer. He went to the hallway, put on his coat and hat, and left.

Elizabeth was worried. Morty usually would say goodbye to Caroline when he left. Marielle had to be up to something. She picked up the phone and called the New York apartment. She let the phone ring, but there was no answer.

Ghani and Marielle were in the middle of making love for the first time. The incessant ringing of the phone interrupted them. Marielle wondered whether she should answer it, but she was lost in Ghani's kisses. About an hour passed when the house phone buzzed shrilly. She jumped out of bed, alarmed. "Who could be here?" she said as she crossed the apartment to grab the phone.

"Mrs. Bennett, your husband's on the way up," the concierge said.

Marielle dropped the phone. "Ghani, my God, you've got to get out of here. Morty's on his way up." Ghani grabbed his clothes putting them on as he ran toward the door.

"No, not that way. Go out the back entrance and use the service elevator." She led him to the kitchen and she kissed him hard on the mouth as she shoved him out the door. She went back to the bedroom. She threw the empty champagne glasses and bottle under the bed and quickly straightened out the bedspread. She went into the bathroom and turned on the shower, stepped in and began to wash her hair.

Morty opened the door, calling her name. She pretended not to hear him and then feigned fright at his appearance. "Morty, my goodness you scared me," she said, covering herself.

"Do you want to ruin us?" he said, angrily. Marielle's heart sank to her feet. How did he find out? Her mind raced. She tried to keep her cool and was about to beg for forgiveness for the affair when he said, "How could you stand up in the United Nations and denounce your own country?"

Marielle was relieved.

"But darling, we are involved in terrible things in Vietnam. I heard it and saw it with my own eyes."

"I don't care what you saw. We are at war. War is hell. Grow up, dear. I work for this government for better or for worse. It's my work for the government which pays our bills. See things as they are, not through rose-colored glasses. Stay away from the UN from now on!"

"I'll do as you ask. I won't go to the UN anymore. Truthfully it's so upsetting and there's really nothing that one person can do. Let's just go to bed and forget all about this. Please." She crossed to the bed, dropped her towel, and slipped under the covers. "Come to bed, darling," she said enticingly.

Morty undressed and climbed in beside her. "You may keep Miriam Hasan as a friend but, please, no more politics," he teased. "What am I going to do with you?" he said as he looked lovingly into her eyes. He pulled her close. Marielle said nothing but didn't resist. She just stared blankly over his shoulder, her mind a thousand miles away with Ghani.

Marielle walked around in a daze during that entire September in 1969. Her childlike trust and awakening to the charms of a skillful lover clouded her judgment totally. Her life stood still. They would often pray together for the good of the oppressed people of the world; Marielle with rosary in hand, Ghani reading from the Holy Koran. He said the book of Allah blessed their love. And essentially it did for she gave herself to him as she had never before with any man. He was her life's breath it seemed as she began to spend more and more time with him.

They met in the most unusual places throughout New York City. Once they went to FAO Schwartz, an exclusive Fifth Avenue toy store, where he bought her a doll for her collection. Another time they sat by a man-made waterfall that was built between two buildings on East 61st Street. They held hands like lovers have done since time began, neither of them seeming to care about the consequences of their love.

One morning they drove to New Hope, Pennsylvania, for a day of walking, talking, and window-shopping for antiques. After looking through the various quaint little shops for a treasure or two, they got back into the car and drove to a secluded campground area. They opened the trunk and took the lunch Marielle packed out of the cooler and put it all into a picnic basket and carried it with them into the woods. It was fun just being two simple people in love. She loved the spontaneity of their relationship. No matter what they were doing it was enjoyable just experiencing the moment together. They walked and listened to the quiet sounds of the forest. Finally, they came to a clearing and spread out a blanket for the picnic.

Marielle sat down and opened the old wicker basket she carefully packed with a delicious lunch of sandwiches and fruits. Ghani brought a bottle of Cristal Champagne. It was his favorite. While a

Muslim by birth, he enjoyed many Western luxuries. The man was a paradox, she thought. He followed no rules but his own.

He deftly popped the Champagne cork and expertly poured it. "Marielle," he said, raising his glass, "You are the most beautiful woman I have ever seen. Your laughter and loveliness have changed my life. I drink to you, to happiness I never thought possible." They clinked glasses.

"I never thought this could happen, either," she admitted. She paused. "I've been feeling very guilty. I'm not free, and neither are you. There are so many people we love who could be hurt by us. The other day when we were almost caught has made me realize we have to stop seeing each other. It's dangerous just being here."

"Never, never. I will never let you go. Somehow we will be together." He began to kiss her. She tried to resist but he grabbed her with such passion it was almost frightening.

"Ghani, aren't you listening to anything I've said?" she stammered as she broke free.

"I don't care what you say. All I know is I want to be with you and I won't let you go. You can get a divorce and come with me when I return to Pakistan later this year. Morty doesn't make you happy or appreciate you like I do."

"But I can't and you're already married twice over."

He laughed, now calming down. "You have such a way of putting things, darling. Those were arranged situations and you know no one could ever mean more to me than you do."

"What about Caroline? I couldn't leave my baby girl."

"Of course, you'll bring her; but this is too much serious talk for such a romantic setting. There is time to plan."

Marielle paused for a moment. "I wish we could be alone together to work this out. There is one special place where we can be together away from prying eyes. St. Maarten. No one is there this

time of year. We could leave this coming weekend. Morty is working and I'll make my excuses."

They did not get back to the city until well past 10 PM. After
dropping her off at her apartment, Ghani returned to the mission.
He knew by the way she kissed him goodbye that she would go to
the ends of the earth if he asked her. He longed to be her prince and
he couldn't imagine paradise being better than when he held her in
his arms.

The next day, Marielle made up some story about friends from
boarding school getting together for the weekend, and off she went
with Ghani to St. Maarten. Marielle knew that her mother suspected her story was a lie because she was furious.

St. Maarten was an amazing little place, she told Ghani, as they
passed the hours of their flight. Being quite civilized, the Dutch and
the French decided long ago to share the precious little jewel of an
island rather than fight over it. The Dutch side was quite proper
while the French side had a nude beach and La Samanna, the most
romantic place to stay on earth.

They were in their own world for those golden days. The sun
shone for them alone, and they were lost in the joy only true lovers
experience once in a lifetime. They ate in their room and after made
love until they both nearly passed out, exhausted by their insatiable
passion for each other.

Marielle took Ghani to the private beach in front of the Bennett
family's villa on the third night. She whispered to him to be quiet, as
she didn't want the servants to see her and know she was on the island without her husband. The moonlight flickered through the
palm trees casting patterns, which danced on her sun-bronzed face.

"When I was young I dreamed of such a woman as you, but
never believed I could have one; and believe me when I tell you if I
should die tomorrow my life would have been full because of this
moment holding you in my arms," he told her.

"I feel the same way. I am ready to leave everything I know behind so I can be with you."

They made love on the sand as the waves caressed their frenzied bodies. Neither one could seem to get enough of the other. Only the light of the morning sunrise made them realize they'd been there all night. No words were necessary as they drove back to the French side and La Samanna.

She was sure it was that night, on that glorious beach, that John Paul was conceived, and it was there in St. Maarten that she and Ghani made plans to be together for the rest of their lives.

She felt guilty for what this would do to Morty. However, Marielle was drunk with the passion she felt for Ghani and not seeing clearly at all. She did feel badly for this betrayal when she stopped to remember how content she was in the early years of her marriage; the Washington parties, seeing her husband speak before the Senate, all the wonderful things she learned as the wife of such an eminent scientist and scholar. She knew that Morty had been a father figure to her in some ways. She and her own father had not been close. She was her mother's princess and was thoroughly spoiled by her.

In her last year at Miss Porter's school her father was killed in an automobile accident caused by a drunk driver. Both Marielle and her mother were devastated by the loss of her father. That fall she went off to Northampton, Massachusetts, to attend Smith College, but on weekends she always went home. Her mother threw herself into the social whirl, and was usually too busy with her society parties to spend much time with her. Marielle knew the loss of her father had been hard on her mother though they rarely spoke of it and Marielle felt very alone and isolated in her grief. She had never really faced what happened or had closure but she knew that Morty was no longer the answer to her happiness or her dreams. She felt trapped and she was well aware that poor Morty was no match for this Don Juan called Ghani Irabi. She was a grown woman now with needs her husband hadn't a clue how to fulfill.

Ghani, too, was being compromised, for he was falling in love with a woman his own people thought of as an infidel. For four happy, glorious days he'd forgotten about his own mission in the arms of the woman he would love for all his life.

Elizabeth knew that Marielle and Ghani had become lovers and encouraged her to break it off. Marielle was afraid to tell her mother how deeply in love she had fallen with him, and that she was planning to leave Morty and take little Caroline to Pakistan.

Ghani said it would be quite easy for her to get a divorce, and that they'd then be married. She was a little bit uneasy about living with his other wives, but his estate was large, and she was so in love that the details about who, where, and what didn't matter; only her passion for this man and the blissful life she imagined they would share.

His kisses, she mused, were the kind one imagines only exist in movies and books. And when he made love to her, her heart almost stopped beating, so great was the excitement and fulfillment.

Morty would surely have noticed, Marielle thought, but it was a very busy and stressful time for him. He was working with Arthur D. Little labs on a delivery system for biological weapons, and the commuting between the Pentagon, the laboratory in Cambridge, and their home in Oyster Bay, Long Island, took a toll. When he was home, he just wanted to rest and play with his precious daughter. Marielle was always pleased that Morty and Caroline had such a wonderful relationship. She was in her own world, even though at times she felt left out. Normally this feeling bothered her, however, she had other things on her mind. Counting the hours until Morty would leave and she would be free to call Ghani and rush to the city to see him.

On Monday morning, after a quiet weekend, Morty was ready

to fly back to Cambridge, Massachusetts, where he was working on a black box project at Arthur D. Little Laboratory. The charged aerosol device they had been working feverishly on didn't spray Anthrax evenly during their last testing, and it had to be perfected for the dog and pony show they were doing for Colonel Haig and his band of Pentagon VIPs who were coming to view their progress mid-week. The kill ratio wasn't a 100 percent yet, and these guys needed to see a clean and efficient kill; not half the beagles surviving. Marielle had been furious that they were killing dogs in the first place. "Why not rats?" she demanded to know. Morty was in a bad mood after the argument they had over it.

Marielle didn't get up out of bed to see Morty off as she usually did. He kissed her on the top of her head; she wondered if it was because she hadn't brushed her teeth yet. *Oh well, his kisses are not the brand to die for,* she giggled to herself. She scrunched under the covers as he closed the door. *Oh Ghani,* she mused, *you'd have kissed me full on the mouth and then some.* She was content to dream of all the little secrets they shared.

The phone rang, breaking the mood. She answered it, as she always did, sweetly and happily. It was Miriam Hasan. Something didn't sound right from the tone of her voice.

"Can you come to the mission right away?" she asked. "It's terribly important. How soon can you leave?" she asked. Marielle was still half asleep. As she paused to stretch, Miriam's voice commanded her. "It's urgent. Please get dressed and come as soon as possible." Marielle, realizing something must have happened, asked Miriam if Ghani was all right. However, the phone went dead. She tried to phone back but got a busy signal.

She was never one to get ready in a hurry. She was meticulous about her hair and makeup. But this morning was different. She was on her way twenty minutes after Miriam called.

As she headed into Manhattan over the Triboro Bridge, Ghani

was all she thought about. She couldn't wait until they would meet again. As she drove, she daydreamed of their four magical days in St. Maarten.

A swerving car jolted Marielle back to reality and she glanced at her image in the mirror. Not too bad, she thought; her hair neatly pulled into a ponytail with a headband that matched her lavender cashmere sweater perfectly. *A cashmere sweater, a pair of slacks, and Gucci loafers are all one needs anyway,* she thought wondering what was so urgent.

Once at the mission she drove into the building garage. They were expecting her as the doors were open and the Hasans' driver was standing there waiting to take her car.

There were several men she never met before and a very tense Miriam waiting for her upstairs.

"Marielle, something terrible has happened. Ghani is in grave danger. Your government and the Israeli Mossad think he is a terrorist directly responsible for the killing of an Israeli intelligence officer called the Ferret. The Israelis are trying to assassinate him for this."

"Did he really kill someone? Or are they lying?" She was shocked and confused by the desperation she sensed in Miriam's voice but, wanting to believe in his innocence with all her heart, she asked nothing more.

One of the men said, "Mr. Irabi is hiding in the Libyan mission on 48th Street. He must get out of the United States as soon as possible. Pakistan can't afford to have an international incident and there are factions in Islamabad who want him turned over to the U.S. immediately."

"Our freighters are docked in Baltimore," Miriam said. "Marielle, I remember you often drive down south to pick up horses, or to attend horse shows around there. No one would think it unusual if you were to drive down there with your horse trailer. Ghani could be hidden inside, and you could help him escape and meet up with our people. You could save his life. Time is a huge factor as the freighter sails Wednesday. He must be out of the city tonight, but it will be very difficult because the Israelis are watching all our allies and their missions."

There was never a question in Marielle's mind as to whether she would help; just how it would be done. *Ghani* must *be saved, at whatever cost,* she thought. How could anyone believe he would take a life in cold blood? She thought of the Israelis and the CIA as a band of rogue agents bent on killing those who would serve the downtrodden people of the world. She believed everything Ghani told her about how these assassins work, even about them killing both Kennedys. She saw herself as a kind of modern-day Joan of Arc standing up for what is right in the face of tremendous odds.

Marielle was also a brilliant and resourceful woman, regardless of what Morty thought. She had, after all, graduated with honors from Smith College, hadn't she? Everyone seemed to be trying to come up with ideas as to how to get Ghani out of the Libyan mission to Oyster Bay Cove, and into the horse trailer so they could leave for Maryland.

Marielle had an idea. She and Miriam and another woman from the embassy would go over to the Libyan mission. Marielle had been there many times for dinner parties with Ghani and was very friendly with the New York Police Department guards in front of the mission. She was a well-known New York socialite and she was also a big donor to many police organizations.

"Listen," she said. "I have a plan. While you ladies walk in, I'll speak to the officers and get them to watch my car right in front. I have a special NYPD parking permit."

Miriam said, "No, Marielle. It's better to get inside. How will you get Ghani into the car without being seen if it's right in front?"

"That's the beauty of my plan," Marielle said. "Ghani will be dressed in the sari worn by whomever we go in with, with a scarf.

No one will notice him. We'll be out in the open and the Israelis won't be looking for him to walk out in plain sight."

One of the men liked her idea. He said, *"Da, da."* It was only then that she realized he was a Russian.

Miriam got Falazir, the wife of the cultural attaché. She was taller than most men and had a face that was long and the saddest eyes Marielle had ever seen. Miriam said she had a very cruel husband who enjoyed beating her. Miriam quipped, "It's not good when they enjoy beating you. It's only good when a wife needs it, don't you agree, Marielle?"

Marielle was too worried about Ghani to think about how prophetic the words of Miriam were about how women are really treated in this world.

Miriam, Falazir, and Marielle were on edge all afternoon. Time passed much too slowly. Three o'clock came, then four. Then, at twenty minutes to six, dressed in their beautiful evening saris, Marielle, in one of Miriam's best that she had borrowed for the occasion, they left for the Libyan mission. Marielle pulled up in front, and as her two companions got out, she placed her permit on the dashboard of the Cadillac Eldorado, got out and approached the police officer on duty in the small booth in front of the mission.

Marielle had a dazzling smile and the young officer recognized her from Earl Wilson's society column. "Hi," she said. "Keep an eye on my car, please. We're going to a dinner party."

Marielle spotted the CIA, or maybe it was the Mossad. Who else would be sitting in a cleaner's truck after 6 PM on East 48th Street? Deliveries were finished by five, trucks garaged and the deliverymen on their way home. She was amused by the obviousness of the surveillance van.

Once inside the mission they were greeted by another friend of Miriam's, an Irish girl named Lisa who worked for the ambassador as a secretary. Lisa's husband, Sean, worked as a bodyguard in Libya for General Khadafi himself. "Come this way," she said, leading them to the elevator. Once upstairs, they were taken to an interior room that was impervious to any outside listening devices.

Ghani was pacing back and forth like a caged cat. Marielle had never seen him so upset. She ran to him. He looked at her and realized how much he loved her. She was everything to him. Her bravery and devotion were so sincere he was overcome with emotion. Not since he was a child had he felt such love for a woman. That woman was his mother.

Marielle explained exactly how she planned to get him to the safety of the Pakistani freighter by tomorrow evening. She wanted so to go with him, but she knew that would be impossible this time. She wanted him to tell her he'd send for her and they'd be together soon just as they planned. But his mind was on other things now and he seemed to be miles away.

Falazir had already changed into other clothing. Ghani needed to put on the disguise, so Miriam and Lisa took Marielle to a conference room where Lisa gave her a detailed map of the Baltimore waterfront area and the dock where the freighter would be waiting.

Then Marielle returned to the conference room and began to put makeup on Ghani. He was fidgeting.

"Hold still, Ghani. If you don't hold still I might accidentally poke you in the eye," she said. She was amazed at how long his eyelashes looked with mascara on them. She decided to keep it to herself. He was too upset to make small talk with her.

"I'm so ashamed for you to see me this way," he told her.

"Nonsense," she answered. "This is real life and I'm here to help you. From now on what happens to you happens to me. Tell me, Ghani, why do the Israelis believe you killed their agent?"

"I must be honest with you no matter what you think of me afterward. I did kill their agent. It was self-defense. They had sent him to assassinate me for standing up for my people," he explained.

"It's all right darling. All people have the right to defend themselves," she stated matter-of-factly. "Don't blame yourself for doing what we all would do if our lives were in danger. I just wish I could go with you. But I know that would be impossible. How will we communicate?"

"I'll find a way to contact you. You must not try to contact me. It's very dangerous now. I hope you understand," he said trying to reassure her.

"Of course, I do and I'll be waiting," she promised.

Several hours had passed since they arrived at the Libyan mission and it was time to get going. All three of them came out, and Miriam and Ghani went directly to the car. Marielle, as planned, walked over to thank the police officer. He asked her if she had a good time.

"Fabulous," she said flirtatiously. "The food was excellent and the company even better. Have a good night and thanks again for watching my car."

As Marielle got into the car she glanced across the street. The cleaner's delivery truck was still there. It said Best Cleaners on it. *They'd better do a bit better,* she laughed to herself. Even she had been able to spot them.

No one followed as they pulled out. *How inept they are,* she thought. *These boys in their black hats just let the cat through the net.* She watched carefully in her rearview mirror as she drove home to Oyster Bay Cove. It had been decided that Miriam would come along, stay over, and have her driver come for her in the morning. Ghani would sleep in the basement bedroom they never used.

Since Morty was still in Cambridge, and Caroline would be fast asleep with her nanny in the next room, the only one to worry about was her mother. And since she was in her own wing on the other side of the house, it was unlikely she'd get up. If she did, Marielle would just say she was having two friends stay over for the night. She often entertained and had guests stay, so it wouldn't seem too unusual.

Elizabeth knew Miriam and was actually quite fond of her. Although she didn't care for Ghani she was always civil when she saw him, so it wasn't a problem in case they should run into each other.

As they got out of the car he smiled with relief at her. How pretty he looked in drag. If he weren't so tall, he'd make a beautiful woman, she thought. They were lucky Elizabeth slept through everything that night.

Marielle began to plan the next day. She wanted everything to go perfectly. She would load up the trailer at 5 AM. It would still be dark out and hard to see the stable from the main house. She wanted to be on the road by 8 AM.

It was now almost midnight. She took a snack to Ghani, wanting to kiss him goodnight. As she walked down the steps to the basement she realized that these might be their last moments alone together. Her heart raced and she was overcome by a feeling of sadness. She was not ready for their time together to end. By the time she got to the basement bedroom he'd already washed off his mascara and lipstick and looked himself again. Their eyes locked, exchanging the silent thoughts that only lovers share. He grabbed her and held her in his arms and they made love, both knowing it might be the last time they would share this beautiful feeling of tenderness and passion, both wanting the moments to last forever.

Morning came much too quickly. Marielle had not been able to sleep. She held Ghani like a little boy to her breast all through the night. Ghani was so exhausted. As the night went on he finally fell asleep feeling safe in her arms.

She was perfect in his eyes and he felt strangely whole and complete when he was with her; a feeling even the causes of Islam did not give him. He asked Allah to forgive him for his feelings; for the fact that Marielle was more important to him than anything had ever been in his life.

Chapter Four

MARIELLE LED GHANI AROUND THE SIDE OF THE HOUSE and down the path to the barn. It was still dark, but she knew the way by heart. He followed close behind her. How wonderful it felt to hold her hand; he trusted her.

She helped him get into the front of the trailer where the hay, saddles, and blankets were stored. She covered him with two extra hay bags and then put the tack trunk in front of him. She even brought one of Caroline's portable potties in case he needed it.

She kissed him softly on his sweet mouth, a mouth that had brought her so much pleasure. How she would miss him, she thought. How awful for him to be reduced to crouching under a pile of hay and horse blankets.

"Dearest," she said, "we'll be leaving shortly. Don't worry. I'll get you safely to the ship." She closed the door, locked it, and hurried up to the house. Caroline and her nanny were in the kitchen. Caroline was always an early riser and precocious for her age.

"Where were you, Mummy?" she asked.

"I've been getting ready to go look at a new pony for you. Sarah Wellington has heard of a lovely Farnley pony that's been outgrown by a little girl and might be just perfect for you next season."

Caroline Bennett, at four years old, had won more ribbons than any other little girl in Long Island history. Her trainer, Mary O'Rourke, of the legendary Rice Farms, said Caroline would be an Olympic champion someday.

Miriam was awake and joined the little group in the kitchen. Caroline's nanny was making breakfast for her and asked Marielle if she and her guest wanted to have some, too. The smell of bacon and eggs made her hungry. Miriam, being a practicing Muslim, said she'd just have eggs and a couple of pieces of toast.

The nanny, whose given name was Aura Rodriguez, didn't mind just being called Nanny. Caroline had started using the name before she could pronounce Aura, and it had stuck. She'd been with the Bennetts since before Caroline was born and Marielle felt like she was part of the family. Marielle had a way of making even those people who worked for her feel good. Nanny loved the family.

It was now half past seven and Elizabeth sauntered into the kitchen. Not much good before her morning coffee, she was surprised to see Miriam.

"I'm going down to Sarah Wellington's to look at a Farnley pony that's just become available for Caroline next season when she starts small pony hunter," Marielle explained. Elizabeth, who had herself ridden the horse show circuit as a girl, loved going to horse shows to see Caroline ride.

"This is rather sudden," she said. "Well, I guess it's as good a time as any to be off and about. Morty won't be back until Friday night and I'll hold the fort down here, dear. Is Miriam going along to keep you company?"

"No. She's going back to the city," Marielle said.

Elizabeth asked how Miriam would get back to the city. She always had to put in her two cents, Marielle thought. "Miriam's driver is coming to pick her up later this morning."

"Well I'm glad to hear that," Elizabeth said. "A horse trailer doesn't belong in New York City. Best for you to go over the Throgs Neck Bridge, through the Bronx, and out over the George Washington Bridge, then take 95 south."

By eight o'clock Marielle was driving down the long, winding driveway, onto Blair Road and out past the Roosevelt Bird Sanctuary, heading toward 107 and the Long Island Expressway. Everyone had come outside to say goodbye. She wondered how Ghani was faring. He'd been under the hay for some time.

Marielle always loved driving, and this time, the feeling was enhanced by the excitement of what she was doing. *Right is might,* she thought, *and how lucky I am to have a chance to help the man I love. This is truly a gift from God Almighty.* As she drove, her mind worked in overdrive, thinking about Ghani, about how her life had changed, about how she hoped she could still share a life with him. How clear her direction seemed on their last day together in St. Maarten. But now there was so much uncertainty.

She stopped to get gas by the Delaware Water Gap. To compound matters, the weather turned nasty, forcing her to drive slower than she intended. It was raining buckets and also getting very foggy. She didn't dare communicate with Ghani. She could only imagine how uncomfortable he must be by now. The drive from Oyster Bay Cove was a long one but even so the time seemed to pass very quickly, and she soon found herself at the Maryland shore.

She wove in and out of the narrow approaches to the docks. Marielle had never been there before. The visibility was extremely poor. There were several buildings and it was hard to see the numbers on them. She became anxious. At every building she slowed up and searched for the number. She had been told to look for building number 12 and that someone would be there to meet her. After what seemed like an eternity of searching, finally, there it was— number 12. She drove to the water's edge and parked. It was

4:15 PM. She looked around and there was no movement anywhere. The foggy haze made it eerie.

She got out of the car and went to the trailer, looking around to make sure no one was there. When she unlocked the trailer door and stepped inside, Ghani looked so tired and disheveled she had to smile. He was such a different sight from his usual elegant and dignified self. They hugged each other tightly.

"Let's go outside for a little air," he suggested. What happened next Marielle would take with her to the grave. In a split second, two people came upon them. She didn't hear them drive up. To this day she doesn't know where they came from.

The woman embraced Ghani and spoke to him in Urdu. Marielle recognized it from having heard Miriam and others use it at the mission. She could not understand what the woman was saying, but whatever it was, it caused Ghani to become very upset. The man, whose voice was indescribable—yet once heard would never be forgotten—sent chills through Marielle.

"Get down on the ground," he growled at her. It was only then that she saw the gun in his hand. In the moment before she could obey, Ghani stepped in front of her, shielding her body with his. "No, Carlos," he said.

"She's seen our faces, Ghani. She cannot be allowed to live." Frozen with fear, Marielle was unable to move or speak. Her legs were trembling. Ghani had his right arm around his back, holding her against his body.

Marielle thought of little Caroline. *My God, what have I gotten myself into,* she thought. The man spoke again. "Step aside Ghani. This business must be done," he said coldly.

Ghani took a deep, long breath. Marielle's heart pounded. Then she heard her beloved say, "Carlos, you will have to kill me too. This woman and her purity are what we're fighting for. If she must die for the noble deed she has done for me, then we are no different from the imperialist swine we are trying to destroy. She must live."

Carlos slowly lowered his gun and put it away. Ghani began to guide Marielle back to her car. The woman stared at her with expressionless eyes. She watched her, then looked to the man for the next move. Marielle was now even too frightened to pray. She was holding up on pure adrenaline.

Ghani was now on her right, still half shielding her as they inched closer to the car. The man came up on Marielle's left so close she could feel his breath against her cheek.

"You have looked into my face," he said. "All others have seen death here in my eyes, the eyes of the Jackal." For a moment his eyes softened and he stepped back. "You may go with your life."

Ghani embraced Marielle. He did not kiss her. "Goodbye my truest friend," he said. "Believe in love, Marielle, for it is the only thing real in this world."

She could never remember how she found her way out of the dock area and back to the highway. She wasn't sure when she began to think clearly again, but she knew one thing; she would try to put the experience somewhere deep in her subconscious and never think of it again. It was too horrible and she just couldn't deal with it at all. She realized that her life must go back to normal as quickly as possible. And she knew in her heart that she'd probably never see Ghani again anyway.

She worried about her family and what they'd think of what she'd done. She hoped they'd never find out. She felt ashamed and floods of tears started to stream down her face. She grasped the steering wheel for support. "Please forgive me, dear God," she sobbed. Finally she pulled the car and trailer over, exhausted, and fell asleep.

A sharp knock on her window made her jump. It was a state

trooper. Trying not to panic, she smiled that southern belle smile she learned from her Aunt Dorothy Lee.

The trooper said, "Now ma'am, don't you know it's dangerous for a pretty lady like you to sleep on the shoulder of the highway?" Marielle's mind raced. She took a deep breath, trying to conceal her nervousness. *Thank God he's not here because of what I have just done,* she thought. *He's just making a routine stop to see why I've parked along the roadway.*

She sighed with relief. "Oh Officer, you're right. I just got so tired I had to pull over. But I'm fine now, thank you. I'm on my way to look at a pony for my little girl, so I'll keep on going. I think I've rested enough now."

Marielle hadn't called the Wellingtons, but she had been down to their farm before. Sarah and Kenny were both fond of her and they'd be happy to see her, even unannounced. At any rate, Marielle realized she had better go through the motions or there would be a lot of questions at home she'd not be able to answer.

Marielle surprised the Wellingtons late that evening and Sarah, who always knew where the best stock could be found, be it ponies or hunters and jumpers, did know of a wonderful little pony, outgrown by its owner, that would be perfect for Caroline. She invited Marielle to stay overnight. They went to see the pony in the morning. She worked out the deal and by early afternoon, Marielle was on her way home to Long Island, new pony in tow. In addition she had adopted one of Sarah's barn cat's new kittens. The little cat was asleep on her lap as she drove home.

Marielle never spoke of what happened; not to Miriam, not to anyone. It was her secret, the darkest secret she imagined anyone could have.

Chapter Five

MARIELLE SPENT THE ENTIRE AFTERNOON OF
September 12th in and out of consciousness reliving her time with
Ghani. She was still daydreaming when Vincent Lancelotti came
into the room and gave her the news she waited to hear. She would
be released from the hospital the following morning. Of course she
would have to take it easy for a few days, at least until they removed
the stitches later in the week. She smiled sweetly in seeming deference to the good doctor's orders, knowing she had no intention of
staying home and resting. Her son and others needed her. She had
been following the news coverage intently, praying for a miracle,
and wanted to be downtown waiting with the other families who
had loved ones trapped beneath the rubble. She clung to the mayor's
undaunted hope that there would be rescues, and never stopped pic-
turing her John Paul and others safe below the street level with air
pockets to sustain them.

It was late afternoon when June came into the room to check on
Marielle. Marielle was awake and began to engage June in conversation. She wanted to learn as much as she could about June's background. Somehow talking to someone with a Muslim background
made her feel closer to John Paul. June was happy to talk. Her shift

was coming to an end and she promised she would come back in a few moments. The two spoke through the evening and into the night, June telling of her childhood and Marielle talking about her son until Marielle dozed off. Once Marielle fell asleep June quietly left the room. She went home feeling good about the fact that she had made a new friend. She was on the early shift the next day and looked forward to seeing Marielle before she left.

Marielle had a restless night. She continually fell in and out of sleep as her mind bounced between the events of the past few days and that September so long ago. She couldn't figure out the relationship between the two, why her mind kept going back to 1969. She just sensed there was something there; something that she couldn't quite place her finger on.

Caroline arrived very early the next morning. Marielle was already awake, anxious to leave the hospital; anxious to find out about her missing son. *How beautiful Caroline is,* Marielle thought. "My precious girl," she said, beginning to cry.

"Please, mother, tears help nothing. Stop crying," Caroline said as she handed her mother a tissue from the box on the nightstand. "Here, dry your eyes. You've just got to be strong and brave for John Paul."

Marielle continued to sob loudly. Caroline did not know how to handle this. She was embarrassed to see her mother so overwrought and on the edge. She was never good at handling emotions in public. "Mother, you've got to get a hold of yourself," she said firmly.

June, who was already back at work and in the process of packing Marielle's med kit, admonished her, "Don't be so hard on your mother after what she's been through. You should be more compassionate."

"This is not your business," Caroline snapped rudely at her. "Look, I know you mean well. I do appreciate your concern but I know what's best for my mother. Please excuse us."

Marielle was sorry Caroline had been so curt, and as she prepared to leave, handed June a note on which she had written her
private number. She squeezed June's hand and said, "Please call me.
I'd like us to be friends. You were there for me through some of the
hardest few hours of my life."

Marielle knew that June felt close to her even though their back-
grounds were worlds apart. "I'll call you soon," June said. "I am
praying for your son. I'm sure he will be found. Keep your faith,
Marielle."

Caroline's face tensed. She hated that her mother needed to be-
friend every stray, animal or human, she came across.

"Come along, Mother," she said, a name she used with Marielle
when she was annoyed at her. She called her Mummy at all other
times. By the time they reached the hospital door, Marielle's car was
already waiting for her. As the driver started to drive toward
Marielle's townhouse on East 64th Street, Marielle asked the driver
to go downtown instead. Caroline knew when to challenge her
mother and was not going to argue this time. New York was still
trying to recover from the shock of the past few days. Businesses
were closed, people were afraid, many having left town. Only police
and emergency vehicles were allowed to drive south of 14th Street.
The mayor wanted to make sure that rescue workers and emergency personnel were able to do their jobs. He knew that hundreds
of sightseers would run to the site of the tragedy if they were allowed to.

Their Mercedes was stopped by the barriers at 14th Street and
Seventh Avenue. Charles, the family chauffeur, drove around in circles, trying to find a way through.

Finally an NYPD captain who had seen them repeatedly came
over to tell them to move on. But by this time Marielle already had
the mayor on her cell phone and, despite his reluctance, had convinced him to allow her past the barriers. She told the captain that

she needed to get through. He apologized, saying that he was just doing his job, but that he had to turn her back. She then handed the phone to the captain. "Please speak to your boss," she said.

"Hello," he said. "Captain Anderson here." When he realized that it was the mayor on the phone, the look on his face was a combination of shock and disbelief. He quickly began moving barriers and getting an escort for their car allowing them to continue downtown. The streets were virtually empty. Whole buildings had been evacuated and the air still smelled smoky.

As they neared the site of the Trade Center the mayor met their car. He was functioning on sheer will. He looked haggard and it was obvious he had had only a few hours' rest since the tragedy. "We are doing as much as we can to find survivors, Marielle. You can't do anything for John Paul here. But we need volunteers. We need boots for the rescue workers. We need help."

Marielle reached into her Kelly bag retrieving her checkbook. She handed the mayor a check for $100,000.

"This will help get supplies paid for," she said. "I need to be here, Rudy. I'm going to send Charles with Caroline to John Paul's apartment to get some of his clothing for the rescue dogs. I need to do everything I can to find my boy." She started crying again and was beginning to get hysterical. Rudy took hold of her and shook her gently.

"Marielle, if you want to be down here you have to be strong and useful. Otherwise you can't stay."

She understood. "Whatever you need me to do I am ready to do it," she said wiping her eyes.

The mayor thought for a minute. "You're wonderful with people; I'll have you help coordinate the volunteers."

"Thank you," she said. "Thank you my friend."

At this point even the eternal optimist mayor knew in his heart that what would be recovered now was going to be bodies—too many to count—and many just in pieces. He had to be strong for the people of the city; stronger than he had ever been before.

His heart went out to Marielle. When he got home that night, he told Howard Koeppel, his best friend, how pathetic it was. Mayor Giuliani was in the middle of obtaining a divorce from his wife of many years. He was also in the middle of a battle with prostate cancer. Howard and his companion, Mark Hsaio, were putting Rudy up during his divorce. They knew Marielle and they decided to go downtown themselves in the morning with Rudy to lend a little moral support to their friend.

John Paul was such a good kid, Howard remembered. But there were so many good kids who were lost in this tragedy. He felt helpless; a feeling the multimillionaire car dealer didn't particularly like, but one that would spread throughout the nation over the next few weeks.

Marielle spent the next few days from morning until night at the site. She coordinated getting supplies of warm socks and boots and leather-lined gloves and wool caps to the rescue workers. The smell and the smoke made her eyes tear constantly and she started to develop a nasty cough. But nothing would keep her away.

There was a sea of faces every morning as people from all walks of life came to do their little bit to get through the grim task at hand. It was arduous work, dirty, dusty hard work, and Marielle threw herself into it. She was consumed by it.

Days became weeks. She got to know the endless stream of faces by name. One man named Juan was looking for his wife who'd been a kitchen worker at Windows on the World. She'd left seven children in Ecuador. They were both in the U.S. illegally so he had nowhere to turn. Marielle felt so sorry for him that she gave him some money and arranged for him to go home to be with his children. At least she would help someone get on with his life.

A young woman named Lauren, whose father was one of New

York's finest, also touched her deeply. She had cerebral palsy and was confined to a wheelchair; yet she came every day. She helped take information and photographs from distraught relatives and people in search of missing loved ones, smiling her crooked little smile as she did her work.

There was a steady stream of local and national politicians, making their visits a combination of concern and photo-op.

Marielle laughed to herself. Even a tragedy such as this gets exploited to some extent. She felt she was on hallowed ground; so many had lost their lives here, and so many more had seen their hopes smashed with the crashing of the towers.

She tried her best to listen to the stories people told her of their loved ones. She always seemed to know when to comfort someone with words, and when to just squeeze someone's hand.

She was amazed so many people came to her to get their questions answered. Finally she realized no one really had any answers. She just happened to be there, and they'd have come to ask whoever was working the booths.

Every day hope for recovering anyone alive dwindled and soon people just hoped to find an identifiable piece of a loved one. She couldn't bring herself to think of John Paul reduced to pieces. Maybe other people but not him. So much pain and no relief in sight. Just more noise, choking dust, and debris.

At night she'd sit in her bath, scrubbing off the day's sweat and dirt. She'd see John Paul's wonderful face and hear his voice in her mind. Sometimes she'd call his apartment just to hear his voice on the answering machine. She wondered if Juan was thinking of his wife or Lauren of her dad. Her mind quickly multiplied the other faces who'd been so helpful in those first few days of the rescue effort. She began sobbing uncontrollably. "I've had enough," she vowed as she dried off and went to bed.

Yet when her alarm rang at 4:45 AM she got up and headed back downtown.

Marielle was an animal lover and befriended two of the rescue dogs, Bingo, an older German shepherd, and Henry, a huge golden retriever with long blond hair. It was Henry who finally found John Paul. He was wearing one of John Paul's scarves that Caroline had brought to the site, a western-type pattern which his owner had let him smell and then had tied around his neck.

Henry was the John Wayne of rescue dogs. He ambled down into the tunnels of debris, quietly doing his job. As usual, Marielle watched the rescue efforts from her station. When a body was found, everything would stop and the rescue workers would gently carry out the fallen loved one, more often than not draped in an American flag.

When she heard Henry's bark, sharp and clear, signaling he had found something, she couldn't breathe. She somehow knew. But there were no more tears left. She had cried them all.

She waited for them to bring forth the body she knew was going to be her son's. Henry came out now and his master walked him back to the staging area. Henry saw Marielle and he started walking over to her. She knelt to hug him. He knew who he had found and they shared a moment of comfort between them. *Whoever thinks animals don't understand humans is a fool,* she thought. *Animals understand some things in a way no human can.* She felt her tears begin to run into Henry's soft fur and muffled her cries in his neck as she held him tightly. He licked her face, and then stood at attention as he always did when a body he had found was recovered.

The mayor and Howard arrived upon hearing the sad news that John Paul's body had been found, and Howard held her hand. Rudy called a young priest from St. Patrick's who blessed the body.

Marielle collapsed and fell to the ground. "Get an ambulance!"

Howard yelled. She was unconscious. The concussion, lack of rest, and the shock of seeing John Paul's flag-draped body had been too much for her. As the ambulance sped uptown toward Lenox Hill Hospital, she flashed back to John Paul, her son, her life.

Chapter Six

THE SPRING OF 1970 CAME AFTER WHAT SEEMED LIKE an unusually long winter, a winter in which Marielle discovered she was pregnant. Caroline loved her new pony, Bam Bam. Marielle was glad about that. She relived that last day with Ghani over and over. How frightened she was by those horrible people. At least Caroline could remember the event as the day she got a new pony. Morty was now spending more time at home since the government abandoned his project at Arthur D. Little.

Her mother spent the spring knitting booties for the new baby who'd be arriving in early June. They were yellow, so they'd do fine whatever package, pink or blue, the stork delivered.

Marielle hardly spoke to Miriam Hasan anymore and rarely went to the city. She was as big as a house with this pregnancy, and her heart was still healing after all she'd been through. She still thought about Ghani and kept a tiny photograph of him in the bottom of her jewelry box. But he had not kept in touch. For all she knew he could be dead. Her heart and body still ached with love for him, but she was getting on with her life. Spring and the Long Island horse show season were getting into full swing.

Marielle was on the committee for several of these shows; one for the benefit of the United States Equestrian Team (USET), called the Highland Horse Show, which was to be held the last weekend of April at the Old Mill Farm on Route 107.

Caroline was showing Bam Bam in the Small Pony Hunter Division for the first time. Mary O'Rourke, Caroline's trainer, was sure the five-year-old would be a champion, and when Mary was sure of something to do with kids and ponies, you could take it to the bank.

Caroline rode Bam Bam to the Small Pony Hunter Championship that Sunday, and the whole family celebrated. Morty beamed for Caroline was the apple of her father's eye.

Meanwhile, Marielle was wrapping up a meeting with the Ladies' Committee at the end of the day. How pleased they all were. Kathleen Ferrill, the committee chairwoman, said they raised $18,000 for the USET. Suddenly, Marielle felt a sharp pain in her back but attributed it to sitting too long in one place. The baby wasn't due for at least six more weeks, but by nine o'clock that night she was clearly in labor and on her way to Doctors Hospital in New York City, the hospital where she gave birth to Caroline five years before almost to the day.

Dr. John Aldrich, her OBGYN, greeted her at the door. "Looks like we're going to have us a baby," he said. Marielle wondered why doctors talked to women like they were little girls, but the steady contractions were strong now, and a retort escaped her as she loudly moaned.

Marielle believed in natural childbirth and had had Caroline naturally. Her coach was Elisabeth Bing, a world-famous Lamaze method expert. Elisabeth would be her coach this time as well. Between contractions, Marielle asked the nurse if Mrs. Bing were there yet.

"Yes," the nurse replied. "She's getting into scrubs and she'll be in momentarily."

This labor was very different from Caroline's. She had labored for about six hours and five-pound, six-ounce Caroline came easily into the world. She didn't even need an episiotomy.

With this baby, however, after ten hours of labor, Marielle was only four centimeters dilated. Dr. Aldrich was getting concerned. Perhaps they should do a Caesarean section. Elisabeth Bing had other ideas. She got Marielle up on her feet to walk around. John Aldrich was a great admirer of Mrs. Bing's, and he agreed to let her try this new method of laboring which she was currently researching for her new book.

"Squat down," she said, "when you feel the next contraction coming." Mrs. Bing was a guru of childbirth. Much as it hurt, the squatting during each contraction provided a form of relief. After about twenty minutes of primitive squatting at each contraction, Marielle got up on the bed and Dr. Aldrich examined her progress.

To his amazement, she had fully dilated during those twenty minutes. He was very impressed. Mrs. Bing was pleased, too. She wanted her work to make labor and childbirth easier for women, and she just saw in practice one of her theories actually work.

"I see the head," he exclaimed. "Push, Marielle, push!" She was exhausted but suddenly she felt her second wind. She pushed as hard as she could. There was little pain; just a huge pressure and then a whoosh.

"It's a boy," John said, as he placed the newborn on her chest. "I'm going to cut the cord now." Marielle could see her baby boy. He was as big as a full-term baby and he had so much coal-black hair it was hard to see his little face. Elisabeth wanted him to nurse before he was even cleaned up. "Bonding," she said, a term most people were unfamiliar with in 1970.

"John Paul. We'll call him John Paul," Marielle whispered. She was exhausted from her ordeal and was falling in and out of sleep as the nurse took her little bundle to clean him up. They did ditto for her and soon she was back in her suite.

The titters and gossip were already beginning as Dr. Aldrich told his father, a retired obstetrician himself who had, in fact, delivered Marielle, that she gave birth to a baby that was dark-skinned and dark-eyed; virtually impossible for two fair, blue-eyed people like Marielle and Morty Bennett. "If I had not delivered him myself, I'd have thought someone must have switched babies."

John's father laughed. "John," he said, "in our profession we see many strange things. Gossiping is not something we physicians should engage in. Make sure you don't say anything to your wife or to your mother. This kind of trivia spreads fast and Marielle is one of the finest young women I've ever known. If she has secrets, let's not help reveal them."

Morty had been waiting for hours to see his wife and new son. As the nurse wheeled in the little crib and handed the baby to Marielle, Morty saw his newborn son, not pink and white with soft blond hair, like his precious Caroline but dark and mysterious. *My God,* he thought, *this can't be my son.* For looking out from under the blue blanket was a child who looked like he'd been tanned in the Palm Beach sun; his little eyes like two deep coals peering out, framed by the longest set of eyelashes he'd ever seen.

Marielle was also in shock, for what she saw was a mini version of Ghani. *Oh my God. Will Morty understand what happened?* she thought. Marielle had only to look at her husband to know. There was a cold hush in the room. He said nothing. He turned and left the room.

Marielle held her son close to her now. He sucked on his little hand. "He's hungry," the nurse said. "Would you like to try to feed him?" Marielle nursed Caroline and enjoyed it. She looked forward to the new baby, not caring whether it was a boy or a girl. The pregnancy actually helped her return to her life. She didn't allow herself to dwell on Ghani and what might have been. She even convinced herself the coming child was her husband's.

As she put little John Paul to her breast, and as she watched him eat his dinner, she knew he was Ghani's son. And in spite of the crisis this was about to throw her marriage into, she felt happy for the first time since Ghani had left.

Forgive me, she thought, *but I am so happy to have our son, mine and Ghani's. I will have a part of him with me forever. In spite of everything now, how blessed and lucky I am.*

Her mother came that evening to see her new grandson. "Well, now you've done it," she harshly admonished. "I won't be surprised if Morty asks for a divorce."

"Shut up, mother. I don't care about anything but my son. Yes I loved Ghani and there's nothing you or anyone else can do to change that."

But Elizabeth underestimated Morty. He truly loved Marielle and he adored his daughter Caroline. He was a man of logic and reason, and once he calmed down from the initial shock of seeing the boy for the first time, he wanted to take Marielle in his arms and tell her he loved her no matter what. He realized, perhaps, that he hadn't given her everything she needed. Maybe he hadn't been there enough for her.

"Good evening, Morty," Elizabeth said when he came in.

"Have you seen our son?" She started to say something, but he cut her off. "Isn't he the handsomest little guy you've ever seen? Don't know who he looks like yet, but the Bennetts had quite a checkered past you know. Kept slaves in Virginia, I'm told. Could be he's some sort of throwback." He laughed it off. "Well our John Paul will be a little black jack."

Elizabeth politely excused herself to let them have some time alone.

Morty took Marielle's hand tenderly. "I love you, my darling, and I love our son," he said reassuringly. "We are a family. That's all that counts. Tell me nothing or tell me everything whenever you are ready. Nothing matters but our family; you, Caroline and little John Paul. You are my life."

She was so touched by her husband's kindness and compassion. And he meant what he said. They never spoke about this again and Marielle was eternally grateful to Morty for that.

As time went on, Marielle and Morty got back into their secure routine. She realized how much she really respected and loved him and how she belonged to this life. It was a good life they had together. Morty won the Nobel Prize for science in 1980, and continued his research work for the government until his death in November of 1999. The hundreds of millions of dollars earned by his many patents were put to good use through the Bennett Foundation helping countless charities and causes.

Caroline and John Paul were both very close to their mother, but there was a rivalry on Caroline's part which John Paul good-naturedly ignored. When they were eight and three, respectively, they were at a large fair and horse show. What happened that day would define their relationship for years to come.

John Paul got lost and while his frantic mother and father searched for him, one of the fair officials brought him back. Caroline was at their show tent by herself. "That's not my brother. He doesn't even look like me," she shouted.

As the man took the screaming little boy away, his parents returned. Morty took little John Paul in his arms, then passed him over to his mother. When her Daddy was told what she had said, Caroline got a sound spanking. "Don't you ever do anything again to hurt your brother," he scolded.

Caroline, angry and hurt, screamed, "But he doesn't even look like us."

Her father looked at her furiously and then he shook her. "Don't ever say that again. Do you hear me?" Then he hugged her close and said, "I'm sorry, my darling, but I want you to love your brother as I do."

Caroline understood. John Paul was different and Daddy and Mummy loved him best. She secretly harbored a feeling of jealousy and confusion toward her brother until the day he died. Somehow she knew in her heart they weren't the same and just his mere existence seemed to negatively impact her life.

There were so many instances of this unspoken problem, this obvious secret, this elephant in the living room. The one time that always came to mind was John Paul's first day of school.

It was a beautiful fall day and John Paul was excited about his first day of school. A charming and bright child, he ran ahead of his parents. Morty called him back admonishing him for not holding his mother's hand. "You're a big boy now and you have to act like a gentleman," he said.

"I'm always a good girl, Daddy, aren't I?" Caroline said, as she squeezed her father's hand.

"Of course you are, Caroline. You are a perfect angel and, John Paul, you're a perfect little gentleman."

Caroline wanted to go straight to her own classroom but Marielle insisted she come along with her family. "But Mummy, I don't want to go to the kindergarten; I want to see my friends."

Marielle ignored her. "Nonsense, Mrs. Jackson will be so happy to see you."

Mrs. Jackson was Caroline's favorite teacher at Portledge. Portledge was an exclusive elementary day school in posh Locust Valley. She taught both kindergarten and music to grades one through three. Rowena Jackson was a real southern lady. She hadn't lost her drawl. She greeted the Bennetts with open arms.

"I've been looking forward to having another little Bennett in my class," she said, her smile turning to surprise as she got her first look at John Paul.

She quickly regained her composure. "Hello, young man," she said patting John Paul on the head. "And Caroline, how you've grown over the summer."

Marielle was used to the reaction most people had when they saw her son for the first time. Morty, knowing the situation well, moved closer and put his arm around Marielle and John Paul.

"Caroline, you never mentioned your parents opened their hearts and adopted a baby brother." Caroline almost wished he were really adopted. That would at least explain everything.

Marielle looked directly at Rowena Jackson. "I beg your pardon," she said. "Our son is not adopted."

The flustered woman didn't know whether to run from the room, apologize, or pretend she hadn't opened her big mouth and inserted her foot. She quickly changed the subject as she began ushering John Paul toward his cubby. "Say bye bye to Mummy, Daddy, and your sister," Mrs. Jackson said, turning her back.

"Mummy, what's adopted?" John Paul asked looking over his shoulder at his mother.

"Maybe Mrs. Jackson can explain that to you later," she said, her blue eyes staring Mrs. Jackson into the ground. Marielle was clearly perturbed.

"Come on, my darlings," Morty interrupted, trying to defuse the situation. "We have to meet Caroline's new teacher."

As they walked Caroline to her class, Marielle said, "I can't believe the unmitigated gall of that woman."

"Let it go. Just let it go," Morty said.

That was only the beginning of the veiled prejudice the Bennett family experienced throughout their children's elementary school years. Even though Caroline resented her brother, she always stuck up for him. She bravely and stoically kept most of the incidents at school to herself with the exception of the day she broke Harry Robert Strouse, Jr.'s nose in the school cafeteria. He was a sixth-grade bully who had been relentlessly picking on John Paul and calling him "brown boy" whenever he had the chance. Caroline was seated at a table among her classmates when she saw him bothering her little brother across the room. He was standing over John Paul's table with his loaded tray in hand.

"Brown boy, brown boy," he said taunting John Paul.

Caroline marched over and tapped him on the back.

"Why don't you pick on someone your own size?"

"Why? Why do you care about 'brown baby?'"

"'Cause he's my brother," she hissed as she wound up and hit him as hard as she could in his face. Blood spurted from Harry's nose as he dropped his tray running and screaming for help.

When Marielle got the headmistress's phone call and was told something awful had just happened, she was frantic. "Are my children all right? What's happened? What's happened?"

The headmistress quickly assured her that her children were fine. However, Caroline had struck a fellow student, and he was on his way to the hospital. She asked Marielle to please come to her office to pick up Caroline, who would be suspended from school.

Caroline was sitting in the anteroom of the headmistress's office when her mother arrived. Her school clothes were splattered with blood. "What on earth happened?" Marielle demanded to know.

"That sixth grader Harry Strouse called John Paul a 'brown boy' and 'brown baby' and I just was so mad I socked him. He picks on him every day, Mummy."

Marielle hugged her daughter. "You're your brother's brave protector. Mummy's proud of you. You wait here."

She opened the door to the headmistress's office without knocking. She closed the door purposefully.

The headmistress addressed Marielle. "Your daughter's behavior will not be tolerated. Poor little Harry—"

Marielle cut her off in mid-sentence. "Harry is a nasty little bully and someone should have stopped him long before it came to this. Poor Caroline, what choice did she have but to defend her brother's honor? Don't my husband and I give you enough money? I really don't care what you think you know. There will be no suspension of Caroline or you can forget the new Bennett gymnasium. Do I make myself perfectly clear?"

"What will I tell Harry's parents?" the headmistress babbled.

"I'm sure you'll think of something," Marielle retorted as she left.

Chapter Seven

DR. LANCELOTTI WAS THE FIRST PERSON MARIELLE saw as she regained consciousness in the Lenox Hill ER. He wanted to say "I told you so" but, damn it, how could he at a time like this. Everyone knew John Paul's body had been recovered. His wife, Gina, had called earlier. Howard Koeppel and Mark Hsaio were planning a small memorial service at St. Patrick's. It was clear that Marielle would be too devastated to manage it. And Caroline and her husband, Patrick, would be busy taking care of her as soon as she could leave the hospital.

Marielle was overcome with grief. Nothing and no one could seem to console her. She relived over and over their last moments together. It was exactly a week before the tragedy. They met for lunch at Windows on the World. John Paul just loved the view and since he worked in the building, it was convenient.

Marielle, for her part, hated the place. It was pompous and overpriced and the food was just so-so. She'd been uneasy just being in the Twin Towers even before the first terrorist attack. The height made her feel queasy and she never dared to look down from the windows. She would always just look straight out.

"Don't you feel just a little bit guilty making so much money this year? You can't really say you've worked for it," she teased. "I don't know why I always imagined you'd be a doctor or a lawyer; not a glorified gambler." She chided him good-naturedly.

"I invest in stocks and bonds, Mother. It's not gambling," he said.

"Well, remember my boy what goes up must come down."

"Not in this market, Mother. The sky's the limit."

"Oh John Paul, my golden boy; whatever you say."

"I haven't talked to Caroline. When is she coming back from London?"

"She's supposed to come in this weekend, and we'll all get together for dinner."

"I don't know if I'm going to be around this weekend, but we'll catch up together during the week. I've made plans," he said, trying to shrug it off.

"What plans? With whom?" Marielle asked, prying.

"I'm seeing some—um—friends, Mother."

"Oh, all right," she said disappointedly. "I guess we'll catch up during the week, then."

"You've got it, Mom." He raised his arm to get the waiter's attention. "The market calls; gotta get back to work," he said, smiling.

Thinking back, she had the feeling there was something he wanted to say, or maybe she was imagining that. She could still see his smile in her mind's eye, and it tore her heart into a million pieces.

Maureen Reilly came by several times to see her, as did June Winters. They both seemed fond of her, but June was more solicitous and eager for the work. During the week Marielle remained at Lenox Hill, June Winters acted as her private-duty nurse. They talked for hours about John Paul. June was the perfect listener and Marielle needed to pour her heart out to someone. June confided that it felt good to have time to get to know someone.

"I feel as if we're becoming friends," she told Marielle.

"We are," Marielle answered. "You have made me feel better

just by being here with me. I can't really tell you why. It's a sad secret from my past, but I'm grateful for your support. More than
you'll ever really know."

June wasn't interested in anyone's secrets. She had her own. She
returned the conversation to a surface topic.

"I usually work back-to-back shifts as there's a shortage of
nurses so I don't have much time for anything else. No romance in
my life."

They both laughed.

"Mine, either." Marielle said.

They watched CNN together both commenting on the
devastation.

"Americans are very lucky," June said. "Even with a tragedy of
such magnitude there are so many agencies to help. In my country
when rockets blew buildings up there was no one to go to. Relief organizations were nonexistent back then. I try to donate a portion of
my salary to Muslim organizations that feed and shelter refugees because of my childhood experiences."

"That's wonderful, June," Marielle said, impressed. "I do a lot of
charity work myself. If everyone felt like we do it would be a much
better world."

Caroline found it strange that the only person who could seem
to console her mother was this peculiar-looking little Muslim nurse.

Marielle hated the forced rest but Dr. Lancelotti said this time
there would be no ifs, ands, or buts. Bored by just lying in the hospital bed, she watched CNN and Fox News coverage of the newly
waged War on Terror, shuffling between the two channels, soaking
up all the news with rapt interest.

"How could these men give their lives in so violent a way," she
wondered. "What kind of God expects true believers to murder
human beings in His holy name?" She said this over and over.

June knew why, and she was tempted to tell her, but decided

just to keep still. *What good would it do anyway,* she asked herself. *No Westerner could understand.* June remembered the American family who had adopted her. She was only seven years old and was so frightened. She never forgot her mother or her father. All the blood running like a river all over the floor. She relived those moments as if they were yesterday.

Marielle lay sleeping and June continued to go over the past in her mind. What was the Red Cross worker's name? She couldn't remember it anymore. She could still hear her saying, "You'll be happy in America." How could anyone have known her adoptive parents would turn her into a virtual slave and not even let her keep her real name. She was so sad to leave her twelve-year-old brother, Ali, behind. He was already running errands for Hamas. She remembered her father and grandfather used to tell her, "One day soon Allah will destroy America and all of Israel." She prayed for that in the Christian Sunday School she was forced to attend.

She thought of how lonely she'd been when Sam left her even though she had married him mostly to get her green card so she could establish her own career. She'd grown used to him. How lucky she was to find her true self again when she joined the Daughters of Mohammed.

She helped raise money for food and clothing and donations sent to Muslim countries. And four years before, she had finally been able to locate her brother, Ali. Since he had a price on his head and was suspected of being involved in any number of terrorist attacks, they were unable to communicate often.

June loved her brother and was proud of what he was involved in. He called her Hana, her real name. They wrote to each other; the letters were carried by hand through the sleeper cells, alive and active worldwide, into the hands of sympathetic diplomats or airline personnel.

There were thousands of such letters transported by extremists on a daily basis, and most were filled with unholy, hateful plans of destruction and terrorism. Few were simply brother and sister separated by war, trying to keep in touch.

Marielle thought she and June were becoming very close. She felt a kinship for her, and she spent hours on end chatting with June about their lives.

After a week, Marielle was finally ready to be discharged. The memorial was to take place on the following Tuesday at St. Patrick's Cathedral. Marielle decided to spend the first few days after she left the hospital in Caroline's penthouse apartment. Caroline had been very persuasive and, frankly, she didn't want to be alone. Patrick was in London and wouldn't be back for a few days. They would have a chance to heal together.

Caroline was feeling terrible for the way she treated her brother. She always felt her mother kept secrets about him and remembered how her grandmother disliked poor little John Paul. She hoped, perhaps, that in this time alone with her mother she'd finally hear the truth about what she hid all these years. Her mother was so overprotective of him. It was obvious to everyone that she loved him so much more than anyone else.

Marielle settled into her daughter's beautiful guest room. It was so inviting, with down pillows puffed up so prettily on the huge bed. The little Queen Anne desk had once belonged to the Duchess of Windsor. Caroline purchased it at the Sotheby's auction. It cost a fortune, hardly worth what Caroline and Patrick paid for it, even though Wally Simpson, the Duchess herself, had sat there and possibly written spicy love letters on it. Caroline also had the little chair that went with it. Marielle laughed to herself, imagining the Duchess farting on the chair. *Oh my,* she thought, *do duchesses actually fart?*

Caroline came in and sat down on the bed. "I'm so sorry, Mummy," she said.

Hearing her daughter speak of their loss was too much for Marielle. She began to cry, then sobbed, "Oh Caroline, I have nothing to live for. My John Paul is gone. My life is over now."

Caroline couldn't believe what she was hearing. At first she felt such sadness about it, but it soon turned to anger as her mother went on and on about how much she loved her son.

"For God's sake Mother," she said. "What about me? Am I nothing to you? Would your life be over if it had been me?"

A shocked Marielle, realizing how much she hurt her daughter with what she said, tried to backtrack.

"Oh Caroline, my beloved baby girl," she said, now sitting up to put her arm around her daughter, "Of course I love you. Truly, truly I do." She reassured Caroline over and over, but she knew the truth. She never loved anyone as much as she loved John Paul, except for Ghani.

Years of therapy hadn't given Marielle any answers for this. It wasn't that she didn't love—even adore—Caroline and Morty. She did love them, but in a different way than she loved Ghani and John Paul. She never felt truly connected to Morty or Caroline. They were reserved and kept their emotions deep inside them. Marielle felt like they were still, deep waters which she could never reach. Ghani was the love of her life and John Paul the product of their immeasurable passion. She had only come to really know herself during her affair with Ghani. She hadn't realized the depth of feeling she was capable of until he touched her soul. After his abrupt departure from her life and the slow realization he would never send for her, she transferred the unfulfilled dreams they shared to her baby son.

John Paul was such a miniature Ghani, it was as if she'd been just a vessel to bring this little angel to earth. She saw no part of herself in him, and she was fiercely protective of him. It was natural Caroline would feel replaced by him, and also that she would have felt the unspoken barrier between her parents as a result of the infidelity, no matter how understanding her father was.

Caroline was still filled with anger and frustration over this, and let loose with both barrels. In a rare explosion of pent-up emotion she screamed, "Tell me Mother, who am I? Did you get me out of a Cracker Jack box? When you stop to think about it, you've never been a real mother to me at all. You idolized the Kennedys and Dad's relationship with them. Christ, you named me Caroline. I'm surprised you didn't call John Paul, John John. Frankly, Mother, he looked more like a Mohammed or a Said. No one had the guts to say it to your face. And Daddy always protected him for you, for whatever reason. I'll probably never know the real truth. But I remember Grandmother calling John Paul the devil's child and trying to get you to have an abortion. I didn't know what that was then, but I knew it must be horrible."

Marielle remembered it well. Morty was in Maryland somewhere in a safe house working on a Black Box Project for two months that fall. It didn't take a rocket scientist, given Marielle's horrific morning sickness, to figure out she was pregnant. Elizabeth had noticed the electricity between her and Ghani early on and confronted her with it.

Marielle was devastated. She put those shaky first few months of her pregnancy and what her mother said to her deep in her subconscious. She closed her ears and her mind when her mother accused her of carrying that "sand nigger's child." Her mother could be as coarse as a sailor.

Like most southern ladies who smile all the time to mask their iron fists in their velvet gloves, her mother didn't mince words with her. As many times as she tried to control her willful and headstrong ways, her mother always ran into a brick wall. Marielle could hear her say how she wished she had been more like she was. She would never have dreamed of doing such a disgraceful and immoral thing.

She had too much pride and respect and love for the old South as she had been taught. The words still stung Marielle even as she recalled them after so many years.

Marielle had truly broken her mother's heart as well as completely disgracing the entire family when she took up with the "coloreds and the riffraff" that changed her mother's way of life forever. Marielle knew she had never really forgiven her for her involvement in "all that civil rights nonsense" during her college years. After all, her mother always said, separate but equal was much better for everyone. "Look at the mess this world is in now because of all that," Elizabeth would always say.

The last straw came when National Security agents showed up on their front doorstep with photos of Ghani. Her mother lied, saying he was only a casual acquaintance and they'd call right away if they heard from him. The agents warned both of them that Ghani was considered to be armed and dangerous. Marielle knew her mother didn't even need to put two and two together. She remembered her running off to Sarah Wellington's and Miriam Hasan being evasive and nervous that morning until her driver picked her up. Marielle remembered telling her she had to relax on her way out. It all fit together. It was so obvious. "A terrorist in our house? Are you crazy?" her mother screamed. "I don't even want to know the details."

"Mother calm down. It's over. He's gone."

"If only God would intervene," her mother said.

"What do you mean?" Marielle snapped.

"This mongrel child you're carrying should never be born. I'm sure the baby is not Morty's. Thank God your grandparents are dead and will be spared such a disgusting scandal," she said repulsed.

"I could never kill an innocent baby, even if it were really the devil's child," she said lashing out at her.

Now she realized little four-and-a-half-year-old Caroline heard them arguing over it. How awful for her daughter. Marielle felt heartbroken, but determined to try to make up to her what she neglected to do long ago; love her. She asked her daughter what could she do to make it better.

Caroline threw the small photograph of Ghani that Marielle kept hidden in her jewelry box on the bed and said, "Well, Mother, for starters you could explain just who this is."

Marielle picked up the yellowed snapshot and lovingly propped it up on the nightstand. She hesitated and drew in a deep breath. "Caroline, that is a man I was once deeply in love with. I made a mistake; it wasn't to be. It was before your brother was born. Your father was very busy and I was very lonely and vulnerable. I met a dashing prince of a man quite by chance, and it swept me literally into a whirlwind of romance and international intrigue. I almost drowned in it and your father rescued me. His strength saved our family from the disaster I had foolishly and recklessly created. I kept the photograph because I did once truly love him. He was John Paul's father."

Marielle once again looked at the picture. *Oh Ghani,* she thought, *how I wish things had been different.* Then she turned to Caroline. "This is the past. It should remain there. Maybe someday I'll be able to speak at length about it, but please understand I simply can't do that right now. I love you deeply my little one. You are all I have left and I beg you to forgive me. Let's put this behind us and move on. Please darling."

"Why should I? Give me one damn reason? You're a liar and a cheat. You've lived a fake life, deceived us all, including my poor father and brother. Why the hell should anyone forgive you?" Caroline said, angrily.

"Caroline, I can't go back and change the past. Why do you think they put erasers on pencils? People make mistakes. People have emotions that sometimes run away with them. Don't you think

I'd have changed this if I could? Please Caroline, I can't handle any-more right now. I need you. I'm so alone, so heartbroken. Please for-give me. I need you to forgive me."

Caroline could see her mother was close to the breaking point and she didn't want to be the one to push her over the edge. She was in enough pain right now. She just had to let her anger go.

With tears in her eyes, she sat next to Marielle, embraced her and whispered, "No matter what has happened, I will always love you, Mummy."

But in reality, Caroline was horrified. All her worst fears were coming true. She was without words. Feelings of disgust came over her like a tidal wave. She wanted to run, but she was afraid of losing her mother forever.

Chapter Eight

As soon as Caroline left the room, Marielle took out the telephone number June Winters gave her. She needed a friend more than ever now; a friend who would really understand, someone from Ghani's world.

June wasn't surprised to hear Marielle's voice on the other end of the phone.

"June, please, I need someone to talk to. Could I come over? Something has happened. I have no one I can talk to." She was mumbling almost incoherently.

June didn't think it was a good idea for her to come to Brooklyn at 10:30 PM. Her neighborhood could be dangerous at that time of night, especially for such a well-dressed lady as Marielle. She told her it was late and asked if it could wait until morning. She'd take the day off and meet Marielle at her townhouse at— say, 9 AM. Marielle was disappointed, but agreed. It was late and June was right. She'd see her in the morning. She hung up the phone and heard Caroline in the hall. Getting up to try to talk to her daughter again, she realized Caroline had dressed and was about to go out.

"Will you be home soon, dear?" she asked, trying to get beyond the angry words that passed between them and hoping that they could finally establish a new closeness.

"Go to bed, Mother," Caroline said tersely. She paused and gathered herself. "I'm sorry for what's happened. I never wished John Paul any harm. I loved him; I truly did." Her voice cracked, choking back the emotion. "And you know I love you too, Mother. I just need time to deal with this, and for God's sake, if Patrick calls, don't tell him about this. He would be mortified and might even ask for a divorce if he knew our dirty secrets. His family would never tolerate a scandal like this. Not now, not ever."

It was just like Caroline to somehow make everything about *her*. Where she got such a self-centered, self-important streak her mother would never know. Marielle was relieved she was gone now, and she just crawled under the covers of the big bed and cried herself to sleep.

Caroline went to her brother's apartment to feed his cat as she had done every day since 9/11. She knew he was seeing someone, because the apartment was strewn with a woman's personal items, makeup, bath gel, etc. But she didn't know who the girl was. She had gone through his Rolodex, but didn't have time to call all the people in it to let them know his fate. She hoped Howard and Mark would deal with his friends. She didn't really know any of them, and wanted to keep it that way. She was now preoccupied with keeping her mother's tawdry past from disgracing her.

When she got to John Paul's building, the doorman acted very strangely and finally said to her, "Lady Harlington, John Paul's girlfriend is upstairs in his apartment. She lived with him, you know, and it's been quite hard on her. She knows he didn't tell his family about her and she just wants to take her things. You understand. She had her own key. I thought it would be all right." Caroline was ready to blow her top after all the recent revelations. Even the doorman had more information on her life than she did. John Paul had a secret live-in girlfriend. *Give me a break,* she thought, *what next?* She walked toward the elevator, ignoring the doorman completely. She didn't care who this girl was, or thought she was. Her brother was dead and she should be supervised, even if the place was filled with her things.

As Caroline let herself into the apartment, she saw John Paul's black-and-white cat, Baby, curled up in this stranger's lap. It was a touching little scene. She was, however, in no mood for this.

"Hello," she said flatly. "I'm John Paul's sister, Lady Harlington. And who are you?" she demanded. The slight figure stood up, facing her. She was a mouse of a girl; certainly not what Caroline would have expected her brother to be attracted to.

"I'm Susan Wentworth," the little mouse almost squeaked. "John Paul always spoke about you," she stammered. "My father knew your father."

Caroline was amused in a weird sort of way. The Wentworths were one of New York's oldest and snootiest families. Imagine how they'd feel to know their precious little heiress was shacking up with the illegitimate son of a "sand nigger," as Grandmother Elizabeth used to call them. No wonder the Wentworths rarely went to social events; Susan was embarrassingly plain.

She asked Caroline if she'd mind if she stayed the night; she missed John so very much. Caroline couldn't have cared less and quickly said, "Of course. Do whatever you want."

Something about Susan made Caroline very uncomfortable, so she put out the cat's food and prepared to leave. Suddenly Susan bolted across the room and grabbed her, bursting into tears and shaking and sobbing.

Caroline gently pulled herself loose and guided the hysterical girl to the big armchair by the window.

"Get hold of yourself," she told Susan. "I'm very concerned about your emotional state." Her words were prophetic indeed.

She sat with Susan for over an hour trying to calm her down.

"Caroline I just don't know what to do with myself. I eat alone. I sleep alone. I don't want to see my friends. I just keep hoping I'll wake up and all this will be just an awful nightmare. I'miss him so much," she babbled on. After a while she just stared blankly into space.

"Are you sure you're going to be all right?" Caroline asked her.

"Yes," she replied not making eye contact and picking up the cat. "You should go home now. I just want to be alone with Baby and John Paul."

Caroline didn't even want to touch that so she left.

By the time Caroline got home her mother was fast asleep. Caroline wouldn't think of waking her to tell her about John's distraught secret girlfriend, and who she was, so she fixed herself a cup of hot milk, ate a couple of sugar cookies and went to sleep herself.

She was abruptly awakened the next morning by the telephone. "Hello," she managed to say half asleep.

"Lady Harlington, this is Clive Reynolds from the Associated Press. Do you have any comment on the suicide last night in your late brother's apartment? Pineapple heiress Susan Wentworth committed suicide there," he said.

Caroline couldn't believe her ears. "I don't know anything about it," she croaked.

"It was quite something," the reporter said. "She jumped out the window, holding a cat. It survived, by the way, and is in the Animal Medical Center. Susan was pronounced dead at the scene."

"I have no comment," Caroline said and hung up the phone in disbelief.

What else could happen? she thought. The phone rang again; it was her husband from London. The story of the suicide was already on the telly there. Patrick told her he would catch the next flight home.

Caroline quickly called information for the Animal Medical Center number. She hoped Baby would survive. Her brother really loved the cat. *If Baby lives,* she thought, *I'll take care of her for you, John Paul.* Caroline realized she was crying for her brother for the first time since the tragedy.

As it turned out, Baby was going to be all right. Her fall was broken by the building's awning and, except for breaking both her front legs, she was unharmed. Thanking the veterinarian on duty for the information, Caroline was then transferred to the business office to give them her credit card information. *Even the pet hospital wants to get paid before they do very much for you,* she thought.

Her housekeeper let herself in and was brewing coffee. "Good morning, Lady Caroline. Would you like breakfast?"

"Yes," she answered. "My mother will be joining me on the terrace. The usual. It looks like it's going to be a warm day." Caroline loved Indian summer weather; those warm few days before the nip of fall takes hold.

Marielle was still asleep when her daughter went into her room and sat on the edge of her bed. She was truly sorry for the things she said the night before, and she gently leaned over to kiss her mother.

"Good morning, Mummy," Caroline said softly. "Please forgive me for what I said to you last night."

Marielle, now awake, reached for her daughter, holding her close. "Caroline, we're the only family left. Let's really try to forgive each other and do our best to make up for the past."

Caroline had the housekeeper remove the morning papers and waited until they finished breakfast to tell her about the latest tragedy.

Susan's suicide note was all over the papers; how life without John Paul was no life for her. It was heart wrenching.

Dear Mom and Dad,

I can't face another day without John Paul. I know I should be strong and try to go on without him. I know you think that's what he'd want. But what about what I want? I am empty. I need to be with him or at least end the pain.

Please forgive me. I don't want to live without him. I can't eat. I can't sleep. I can't even put one foot in front of the other anymore. I'm so sorry for hurting you. I love you. Baby and I are just too lonely for him. Goodbye.

Your loving daughter,
Susan

Marielle's heart went out to the Wentworths. She wondered if they'd been in the dark about the relationship as well but she was too grief stricken to admit to herself that as John Paul grew into a man they weren't really as close as they once had been. She always knew what the right thing was to do and even though it was hard on her she called them and suggested John Paul's memorial include Susan and that perhaps the lovers be buried together.

The Wentworths, both reclusive individuals, thanked Marielle. It did seem appropriate, somehow, under the circumstances.

The Bennetts had a family tomb on their 300-acre farm in Massachusetts. It was decided that, after the memorial at St. Patrick's, John Paul and Susan would be laid to rest there in the mausoleum. The memorial service was very simple and beautiful. Caroline asked to speak. What she said brought tears to everyone's eyes.

"Life can be gone in a moment, so show your love every day. I never told my brother how much I loved him; now I will regret my whole life what could have been. I only met Susan once. John Paul and Susan didn't feel close enough to their families to share their love with them. Don't let this happen to you. Show your love, for in the end it's all any of us has."

Marielle was too overcome with grief to speak. She barely heard the condolences of the stream of politicians and community leaders whose careers had been built by her generous contributions and support over the years. Mark Green and his wife, Deni, tried to comfort her but it was just a big, sad blur.

After the service she got into the limousine for the long ride to Massachusetts and Rose Heath Farm. Lily and Cabot Wentworth rode with her, as did Caroline and her husband, Patrick. United in their sorrow, the families rode pretty much in silence, pondering their own quiet thoughts, enduring this first bit of hell before their prides and joys would be ensconced forever in the cold granite walls of the tomb.

The sun flickered its golden light through the massive pines that sheltered the Bennett family tomb. *It is such a beautiful resting place,* Marielle thought, as the limousine came to a stop.

Father Sirois, the family's spiritual advisor, was already there and he began his sad duty. The coffins were placed inside the sleeves of the tomb and the priest's words were lost to Marielle as her grief overwhelmed her.

Everyone had left by now, and she just stared in silence. "You must let go," he said.

"I can't, Father. I've lost my John Paul."

"But Marielle, he was not your John Paul. He is God's and God has called him home."

"Please, Father, go up to the house. Help the others. I need some time to be alone here."

"Poor Marielle," he said. "Don't become a prisoner of the past. Let him go."

But how can I, she thought. *How can I ever do that?*

As Father Sirois walked away, the memories of her son flooded her with the pain of her loss. They burned her. She relived 9/11. "Oh son," she sobbed, "did you suffer? Were you frightened? Did it happen in an instant?" She prayed it was mercifully quick, before he realized he would die. She couldn't bear to think he knew what was happening.

She remembered the body parts all over the West Side Highway and relived the carnage. "Dear God in Heaven, how can you let these things happen? Is there really a purpose for something like this? Are you punishing me God for my infidelity? Is that why you took my son?"

The possibility of her guilt gripped her soul. "Forgive me, God. Somehow I'll make it right."

The falling of the buildings played and replayed in her mind. Over and over. She placed her hand on the cold granite, freshly sealed, and wondered if John Paul was cold. He was beyond her ability to comfort him. She remembered how she would kiss his boo-boos away when he was a little boy.

"John Paul, I promise to avenge your death somehow, if it's the last thing that I do. My sweet little boy who never even knew his real father."

Then she began to imagine a different life: Ghani knowing his son, John Paul bouncing on his knee. She felt sure they would have adored each other. "Oh God, there is no rhyme or reason! Help me! Help me."

Then she got hold of herself. She kissed John Paul goodbye through the granite walls, the cold stone on her lips. "Farewell, my son. May God bless you and protect you forever."

Walking up the wooded path toward the old farmhouse, she vowed to right these terrible wrongs for all the mothers, fathers, and sons—someday, somehow.

Lily and Cabot Wentworth spent about an hour at the farmhouse, going through old albums with Caroline; books filled with photographs of the Bennett family. Lily started to cry, which was very disturbing to Cabot as he came from the old school of controlling one's emotions at all cost. She told Caroline that she must have failed Susan for her to have taken her own life. Why she chose to follow John Paul into the grave rather than turn to her family for comfort is something she'd never know.

Caroline saw the tragedy even more personally and wondered if she could have stopped Susan had she only been more caring that night at John Paul's apartment. September 11th took more lives than those at the Trade Center. She would never be the same.

The Wentworths, my mother, Christ, she thought, *too many lives to count, all forever changed by one senseless, brutal act.* She tried to find something comforting to say to Lily but words were hard to come by. After a few minutes of silence, all Caroline could do was inquire if they had ever met her brother.

To her surprise the Wentworths said they had been very close for a little over a year. Caroline immediately remembered that it had been just about that time that John Paul moved away from home. She made a mental note never to mention that fact to her mother. It would be too upsetting to her. That he kept such secrets from her would be too much of a betrayal. She was lost in her own thoughts when Lily began to speak.

"We thought John Paul was such a wonderful young man. They were planning to run off and get married. He was just so afraid your mother wouldn't like Susan. He told us she didn't like any girl he liked. Isn't that silly and unimportant now? At last they are together," she said, breaking into sobs.

Caroline understood even more how her mother smothered John Paul with so much love there was no room for any woman except her in his life. Her marriage had been a priority for her mother. She had been tossed from the nest with the first available, suitably titled bloke, while her mother had been furious when her brother had gotten his own apartment. She sulked for weeks because he didn't give her a key. She could still hear her mother saying, "Why does he need more space, for goodness sake? He's got a whole floor here; and who will look after him? How will he eat if Cook doesn't make him dinner?"

Just recalling that drama made Caroline sick. She would always know she was second fiddle. She loved John Paul dearly and was slowly beginning to see that none of what happened was his fault. She resented her mother for causing such a wedge between them, but even that was water under the bridge. She wanted to get beyond herself and her feelings so she could comfort Lily.

"Is there something I can do?" Caroline asked, the words sticking to her lips.

"I have nothing," Lily sobbed, "nothing."

"Come on, dear," Cabot said. "Let's get on our way home."

Raising her voice, Lily said, "What home, Cabot? We have no home. We have nothing now that Susan is gone. Just emptiness, that's all." Her sobs became wails as she walked out the door to the waiting limousine.

"Excuse my wife," he mumbled. "She is very distraught."

Caroline hugged Cabot. "Please get back safely. Feel free to come here to visit Susan whenever you like. She and John Paul are together now in Heaven. They truly loved each other beyond this earth." He said nothing, but just turned stoically and got into the car.

Caroline wondered what Lily meant when she said, "We have no home." Death is supposed to bring families closer, not tear them further apart.

On Monday morning in the *New York Post* on page six Caroline saw that the Wentworths were separating after a thirty-year marriage. She was sorry for them, but that was life nowadays. People broke up more often than they stayed together.

She marveled at her father and mother, and how he kept their family together through events that most men would have balked at. Morty Bennett had been an extraordinary person and Caroline admired and loved him for it. She missed her father so much. She wondered if her mother ever missed him as well. She would ask her when the time was right.

Only time would heal this, too. Baby, the cat, was out of the hospital. She would make a full physical recovery, but Caroline was sure she missed John Paul; probably not Susan after what she had done. Caroline couldn't help but laugh. The poor cat must have freaked as that girl tried to kill her. Baby wouldn't go near the terrace or the windows, and would scratch the hell out of anyone who tried to pick her up. She put new meaning into the word "independence" as it related to cats.

Caroline was determined to make up to John Paul all the years of jealousy and indifference by caring for his beloved, totally neurotic cat. She also decided to try to forgive her mother for things that happened long ago. They really had nothing to do with her. She suggested her mother join her and her husband in St. Maarten for a much-needed rest.

She wanted to plan a living memorial for John Paul as well; through their foundation that would help the surviving families of the Trade Center victims. It would be something that would help them heal and bring her closer to her mother; something she wanted more than anything in the world. Now that the funeral and burial were over, it was time for a new page to be turned in the book of their lives.

Several weeks passed. The memorial service at St. Patrick's had been the last time June Winters saw Marielle. She had not wanted to bother her, and had decided to just sign the register and not try to approach her. There were so many people there, and she felt out of place. She prayed to Allah for John Paul and his girlfriend, Susan, hoping they were in Paradise together.

She hadn't heard from Marielle. She wondered if she'd ever hear from her.

Then she got a letter from her brother, Ali. It contained a sealed letter with the name "Marielle" on it. Her brother asked her to deliver it to her.

She had written Ali about how she had taken care of internationally known socialite and philanthropist Marielle Bennett after her son, John Paul, was killed. But why would Ali ask her to deliver a letter to Marielle?

She was tempted to steam open the letter with her teakettle, but in the end she decided not to.

She called Marielle's private number and got a recording *"Hi. Leave a message and I'll call right back,"* it said. *No one could mistake that sweet voice,* June thought.

"Marielle, it's June Winters. I'd like to come over to see you when it's convenient. I have something to give you. It's very important. Please call me as soon as you receive this message."

Chapter Nine

ST. MAARTEN WAS, AS IT HAD ALWAYS BEEN, AN OASIS from the pressures of life. Even when a hurricane hit the island a few years back, their little villa was virtually untouched. La Samanna was hit hard as were other properties on the French side. Marielle marveled at the power of nature. The sea, so calm and serene, could be whipped into a frenzy in moments by the relentless winds that could rip buildings from their foundations in seconds. *Mother Nature is a bit of a terrorist herself,* Marielle thought.

Patrick was a late sleeper, but she and Caroline always awakened with the dawn. They'd hear the waves licking the sand on the endless span of beachfront. They'd get up, make tea, and then take a long, leisurely walk together, singing their favorite old songs and running in the surf, enjoying the feeling of the sea kissing their ankles, toes squishing in the wet, mushy sand. There was so much to be thankful for even in light of their terrible loss. During one of those walks Caroline confided that she was expecting a baby.

"When are you going to tell Patrick?" Marielle asked, pleased that she had told her the wonderful news first. The thought of the new baby gave them a bittersweet bond.

"Soon, Mother, soon," she replied.

Marielle sank onto the sand. Caroline sat beside her and they watched the sunrise.

"Caroline, I know there are some things we can't make better. I realize how selfish and self-centered I've been in my life, and how much I may have hurt you. I'm so sorry, dear. I guess I just didn't know how to handle my life. I was too sheltered as a teenager. Your Grandmother Elizabeth did what she thought was right and then Smith was—well there weren't any boys there." She laughed.

"Your father was too old for me, and we weren't—how shall I say it—so compatible in some ways. He was a good and kind man, but he wanted a Stepford wife, not the sensitive free spirit that I was inside.

"The affair should never have happened, but after it did, I created a dream world with the son of my dream lover. John Paul became my focus, and I'm afraid I neglected you. I didn't realize it at the time. I truly always loved you, and now I can only tell you once again how much I hope you will forgive me."

Caroline was touched by her mother's honesty. "Mother, there is nothing to forgive. We are both grown women and we need to follow our hearts. We've both got to try to forgive ourselves and do better in the future. I'm about to become a mother and frankly I'm scared to death that I won't be any good at it. People aren't perfect, so give yourself a break. I miss John Paul too, and I have my own regrets. Now let's go back to the house. I'm hungry. How about you?"

"I'm starving," Marielle chimed in.

"I'll race you," Caroline said.

"You're on, kiddo," she replied as she took off, her long legs kicking up the sand.

Marielle beat Caroline back and as they climbed the stairs to the breakfast deck, Caroline teased her. "You're not such a big deal—you beat a pregnant gal." They laughed heartily.

"What's so funny?" Patrick said, looking up from his newspaper. He was still in his pjs.

"Nothing, darling," Caroline said. "Just mother and daughter stuff."

"When are you going to tell him?" Marielle whispered.

"What are you two cooking up?" Patrick demanded to know.

"Well, if you must know the secret," Caroline beamed, "I'm the one who's cooking as they say over in London. I've got a bit of bun in the oven."

"What?" Patrick exclaimed. "Are you, I mean, are we? Oh my God, Caroline, my darling, that's just fantastic. A baby. Sit down dear, you must rest."

"Patrick, I'm not tired," she said, laughing, "I'm just pregnant."

The time flew by and before they knew it they were on an American Airlines plane heading back to New York.

Once home, Marielle caught up on her correspondence and made a note to call June. After looking all day for the number, she finally called Lenox Hill Hospital.

"Sorry, we can't give out the home numbers of our personnel."

Annoyed now, Marielle called Carrie Lane over in the fund-raising office. Carrie was happy to hear it was Marielle Bennett on the line. She was one of the hospital's major contributors.

"Hello, Marielle," Carrie said. "What can I do for you?" Marielle told her about not being able to find June Winters's number. Carrie said, "Don't worry. I'll get it right this minute. I'll call you right back." It took Carrie exactly seven minutes to get in the elevator, rush down to records, bring June Winters up on the computer and call Marielle from her office.

Marielle called June and told her how she had to go through a lot to get her number as she somehow misplaced it. They laughed. They agreed to meet for lunch at the Italian restaurant run by

Grace's Market on Third Avenue and 71st Street. Marielle wanted to pick up a few things at the market anyway.

The two women hugged each other and sat in the back of the restaurant where it was quiet and they could talk. June felt she could trust Marielle, but even if she hadn't felt that way, she would still do what her brother, Ali, had asked her to do.

As they sat down to lunch, June began telling Marielle about her life. "I was an orphan, you know. I was born in Lebanon and adopted by Americans through a Red Cross program." Marielle wondered why June was telling her this again, but she saw how earnestly she was speaking, and how important it seemed to her, so she politely listened.

"I have a brother," June said. "His name is Ali. We found each other a few years ago, and now we keep in touch. I wrote Ali about you; I mean I told him what a fine woman you are and—well, I don't know why, but Ali sent you this in his last letter to me. I don't know who it's from, but he asked me to place it in your hands."

June reached across the table and gave her the letter. Marielle looked at her name written on the sealed envelope and knew instantly who wrote it. Visibly shaken, she couldn't finish eating.

"June, let me get the check. I want to go home and read this. Thank you for bringing it to me. I can't stay. I want to go home and be alone. We'll speak soon." Marielle put forty dollars on the table and left, clutching the letter. She returned to her townhouse with haste.

Overwhelmed with emotion, in the quiet of her study, she read.

> *My Darling Marielle,*
>
> *It has been thirty-two years since you risked everything for me. I have wanted you and thought of you every day during those years. My personal destiny was, however, to fight against the Zionist imperialists who, even as I write this to you, kill and maim my people and prevent us from*

raising our children in our God-given homeland. I have dedicated my life, the life you saved, to Jihad.

As you rebuilt your life, I built many organizations dedicated to the destruction of the enemies of Palestine. With each successful mission I have praised Allah for it brings us closer to our victory. But it was with great sadness that I learned one of your children died with our martyrs on 9/11.

If I could give you back that child I would cut off my hands, but the child is now with Allah.

I wonder if you remember the love we shared once. You are a widow, and the other child, Caroline, is grown. If you still hold me close in your heart, come to me. It will all be arranged and we can spend the rest of our lives together.

With only love for you in my heart,
Ghani

Marielle realized at once just what this letter implied. She froze. *Holy Mother of God,* she thought, *if I had not saved this man and the Israelis had succeeded in killing him, thousands of innocent lives would have been spared.* Could it be possible that he was one of the architects of the infrastructure of worldwide terror organizations? The consequences of her act of love tore at the core of her soul. And at the same time, she realized that God himself was giving her the chance to redeem herself.

After the initial shock of it all wore off, Marielle began to think of what she could do to right such a terrible wrong. *My God,* she thought, *while the world is chasing Osama bin Laden and Mullah Omar, what if they are just small spokes in a giant wheel that Ghani Irabi has created?* He was considered a major threat thirty years ago, she remembered. When the National Security Agency was hunting for him so they could turn him over to the Mossad. Morty had said he was thought to be the head of an international terrorist conspiracy.

"Thank God he's out of our lives, and did us no harm," he said many times. Marielle felt dirty and ashamed. Surely Morty suspected that he was the one. She wished she could've been strong and resisted the affair. Morty's words always haunted her and now she felt she had to do something about Ghani immediately.

Marielle was not without resources. She placed a call to her senator friend, Teddy Kraft. "Senator, it's Marielle Bennett. I have some vital information for the Senate Intelligence Committee. I can be in Washington tomorrow morning if you can get the members of the committee together to meet me."

Everyone knew Marielle Bennett, but the senator wondered what on earth could she know that could be vital to national security.

Marielle also called Mike Adams, another friend who was a Washington insider, a former director of the National Security Agency. They became close when she worked on the committee for Caspar Weinberger's fund-raising dinner, which had been held, ironically, at the World Trade Center several years before. Morty often made Marielle chair Republican events to further bolster his standing with the military establishment. His research funding depended on their largesse.

"What a surprise," Mike Adams said as he recognized her voice. She told him she had a letter that could be very important to national security and a story that might even shake their long relationship of friendship and trust. Later that night Mike told his wife he was worried about Marielle. He thought she might have gone off the deep end over her son's death.

After hanging up with her, Mike got a call from Kraft. The senator started to tell him about Marielle's call. He said, "She called me too. . . . No I don't know what to make of it but, I'll be there tomorrow morning. Let's take this up at the vice president's residence, shall we?" Mike suggested. "The Cheneys are away, and it's private. You call the members, but don't say too much. I'll arrange to pick her up at Reagan International and see if I can get to the bottom of it before she meets with the other senators."

Kraft was relieved. At least he didn't have to pick her up, and if she really had some kind of hot potato, who better than the NSA to cool it off? They knew what was what, which *I*s didn't get dotted and which *T*s didn't get crossed.

Marielle drove herself to the airport. She had been up most of the night. When the plane landed in Washington, an official government SUV came out to the tarmac to escort her with Mike waiting inside. He hugged her, gave her his personal condolences, and asked her to tell him just what she had.

They sat for a long time as she told him what happened thirty-two years before. Then she showed him Ghani's letter and told him about how she planned to bring him to justice.

Mike was not one to let anything shake him, but these revelations by one of the most respected American women would take some digesting. The letter was probably the hottest piece of intelligence concerning the Middle East he had ever seen. It was definitely too hot for the Senate Intelligence Committee.

He called Kraft. "It's nothing. Cancel the meeting. She's going through some kind of post–9/11 stress due to the loss of her son."

Marielle was upset by this.

"Marielle, get hold of yourself. This is the kind of stuff that could get you killed. This is an 'eyes only' document as of this minute. You are not to speak about what you just told me to anyone."

"I'm going to send you over to the house to stay with my wife. I'll show this to the CIA and then we'll set up a meeting. You can tell them your ideas about how to bring down this Ghani Irabi. My God, no one knows that name except people with Q Crypto clearance. We know very little since he disappeared over thirty years ago. We do know that there exists somewhere in the Yemen desert a vast secret complex which we believe to be world Islamic terrorist headquarters. These are the most dangerous people on earth. Even the Israelis have no handle on this bunch."

His wife, Jeannie, was happy to see Marielle. She wondered why Mike didn't let her know they were coming, but the "general," as she called him, did things his own way.

"Don't let her out of your sight and Marielle, do not use the phone," he said before dashing back to his office. Mike then met with the deputy director. "Jesus Christ!" was all he could say.

They scheduled a meeting with Marielle for later that afternoon. The various assembled department heads were shocked when she related how she had helped Ghani escape, and about her face-to-face encounter with Carlos the Jackal.

The first man to speak was the perfect poster boy for the marines. His sinewy hands moved back and forth as he addressed the group. "Ghani Irabi is probably the least known and most dangerous man alive. The Israelis have a lot more data on him, but we do know he has built some kind of underground fortress in Yemen. From there he directs worldwide operations for every Muslim terror organization operating today. He handles the distribution of funds and is a member of the most trusted inner circle of advisors to the Saudi royal family.

"All attempts so far to penetrate this complex have failed. The Israelis have lost agents in this process and, off the record, so have we. They have an ESP about the secrecy of this place we've code named 'Hell.' Even the slightest chance we could take this place out would be worth whatever human cost we'd commit to it."

Marielle would later know this man as Red Connors. He

would become her mentor and friend, and would also be responsible for preparing her for the real-life Mission Impossible she would undertake.

She pointed out that from what Ghani said in his letter, she could soon be living with him; and if he spent all his time at this place she'd probably be there, too. But when she began to detail how she wanted to assassinate him herself, and how she could destroy his entire conclave, all ears were strained not to miss a single word.

"He wants me to come to him. I am prepared to do just that. In what must be a coordinated effort with the Israelis I will, somehow, assassinate him with a device you will give to me that, once detonated, will destroy the entire complex."

One of the men said incredulously, "Are you saying you're preparing to undertake what can only be a suicide mission?"

"Yes," she said, confidently. "How else can I repair the damage I did when I saved his life? So many have died because of me, including my own son. He was Ghani's son you know. He killed his own son with his misguided fanaticism, the son he never knew he had."

Most of the hardened intelligence officers were sympathetic to this beautiful and powerful, yet vulnerable, woman. But one of the senior field agents, Don Haley, was less than enthusiastic.

"I think you've all lost your fucking minds. We can't even get a trained operative anywhere near this place. The Israelis haven't fared much better and you brilliant idiots are going to send some fluffy, stupid little well-intentioned socialite to their complex to alert the bastards that we now definitely know where their headquarters are. Not since we paid all of Khomeini's expenses in Paris, came up with the great idea of giving the Shah cancer, and put our own puppet into power—and you all know what happened there—have I heard a more absurd plan. But knowing you guys, this is probably the plan we're going to end up going with. Well, you'd better start training the lady."

Marielle was angry. She felt they weren't taking her seriously. "Listen, I have financed more senators' careers on Capitol Hill than there are assholes in this room. If you think I'm a fluffy piece of empty-headed cake you'd better think twice. I probably know more about the U.S. military arsenal than all of you pompous full-of-yourselves gentlemen put together. My late husband designed and invented most of it."

"Damn it to hell," Red Connors said. "The lady seems to have a pretty solid plan. You know this Ali al Ilani? He is a planner at Hamas as well as having been involved with the founding of Al Aksa in Frankfurt. He is also a double agent for the Mossad. How did we get so lucky?" He laughed. "Once she's in, it will be our job to get the device to her."

"If we could get the device into that compound we wouldn't need her," another participant commented. "Hell, this is like trying to bell the cat. She'd have to take it with her and it would be discovered. So let's go back to the drawing board, gentlemen."

Marielle remembered an abandoned project of Morty's that had to do with a thin, plastic material that could house sophisticated explosive triggers so they would be virtually undetectable. She could carry the trigger disguised as something in her makeup case, using Dr. Bennett's thin plastic film to mask the device.

"I have kept all the private, hand-written papers that Morty worked on; even those concerning Black Box Projects. It would take a little looking, but I'm sure I have them somewhere, and maybe even a sample of the film," she said.

"That won't be necessary," said Colonel Haig, one of the observers and an old colleague of Dr. Bennett's. "His project was never totally discontinued. We've got the material and we are currently testing it out at White Sands. This seems as good a time as any to see if it's going to work."

Chapter Ten

THE FIRST ORDER OF BUSINESS WAS TO OBTAIN SECURITY clearance for Marielle. As soon as that was done, a small group of key agents responsible for her training was called together for a briefing. She was advised to go back to New York and continue to build her friendship with June Winters. Israeli military intelligence and high-ranking members of the Mossad were notified and were en route to Washington. Leron Yitzaki would act on behalf of Israel.

When Yitzaki was briefed prior to leaving Tel Aviv he listened with great interest for it was he and two colleagues, now deceased at the hands of the PLO, who had sat in the Best Cleaners van that night so long ago. He remembered the incident too well. All three of them made comments about what a dish Marielle was. They didn't know her name then but Yitzaki took pictures of her, as they photographed everyone who went in and out of the Libyan mission.

He ordered all the photos from that September 1969 night brought from the archives. He had to see how they missed Ghani Irabi if, indeed, he walked out with Marielle.

"Here's the file, sir," his secretary said as she handed him the photos and surveillance notes from long ago. When his El Al flight was in the air he began to review the file. He was unable to pick out

Ghani; it looked like three women. Nothing unusual except the one woman's special privileges with her car, and the distraction of her walking to the police booth. There were no photos of the other two getting into the car; just Marielle talking to the officer, and then her driving away with her passengers who looked like two normal Pakistani women.

Leron hated this woman and what she had done. If it were up to him she'd be cancelled. *What on earth,* he thought, *can the CIA be up to that concerns a mission involving her?*

Men like Leron see things in black and white only, never grey. Either you are for Israel or you don't make the alphabet and are the enemy.

Leron and his family had lived in the settlement Alei Sinai in the Gaza Strip for years. It was always a hotbed of Palestinian terror activity, terror that enveloped everyone; men, women, and children. *No one can feel safe there,* he thought, *and it's because the West won't allow Israel to crush these Palestinian cockroaches once and for all.*

Leron had been to Langley, Virginia, and had a couple of buddies within the agency. He hoped that maybe they could take in a hockey game or two while he was there.

As he entered the building and showed his ID, he was surprised at how things had changed. *It's about time these guys lived in the real world,* he thought as he saw the beefed-up security in place since 9/11.

Once inside the briefing room, he watched a surveillance video of Marielle spilling her guts. But it was the letter that really piqued his interest. *The elusive Ghani Irabi was just like any other man, thinking with his dick. He obviously trusts Ali al Ilani a lot more than anyone imagined.*

"Ali is a decent guy," Leron told his U.S. operative counterparts. "We captured him years ago. His wife needed a kidney during his imprisonment. She came to visit him all the time. She fainted on the floor of the prison waiting room one day and was taken to the hospital. The Israeli doctor felt pity for her and there was an organ available from a mortally wounded Israeli soldier. There was no other match for it, and in his compassion for the woman, Dr. Simcha Ron saved her life. After she recovered she convinced her husband that the Israelis were good people, and that peace was best for everyone.

"Ali was then given amnesty and he began to provide us with vital information. He saved many lives and as he became more powerful within Hamas our intelligence community began to value him as a trusted agent. He has been trying to infiltrate the upper echelon of the Al Qaeda for a number of years now, and when his sister wrote and told him she was taking care of a famous American socialite, he shared that information with some of his associates.

"One of the men was a close confidant of Mullah Omar and Osama bin Laden's. In a meeting at the secret headquarters of Ghani Irabi's giant network, the men talked about 9/11.

" 'Oh yes,' said Ali's friend Abdul. 'Ali al Ilani's sister in New York is a nurse and one of her patients, a prominent American socialite, Marielle Bennett, lost her son in 9/11.' They smiled. 'It is good to know we have hurt these Americans, rich and poor. May they suffer for eternity,' Abdul said.

"When Ghani had overheard Marielle's name, he rushed over to Abdul.

" 'Who told you this story?' he questioned.

" 'Oh one of our plants; a mid-level soldier in the Hamas.'

"Ghani said, 'Bring that man here immediately. I want to speak to him.'

"Ghani's interest did not go unnoticed, but no one inquired as to why he was so interested in the man or his story.

"When Ali was brought to Ghani he explained, 'Marielle Bennett is someone from my past. I am going to write a letter to her.

Will your sister give it to her? I mean I want her to place my letter directly into Marielle's hands.'

"'Yes sir,' Ali said. 'I know my sister will place it in her hands.' He waited for the letter to be written, and the envelope sealed, and then took it and included it in his next letter to his sister.

"Ali did not tell the Israelis about the letter, but he did tell them that he had come to the attention of the supreme leader of the Islamic movement. He said he didn't know what his role might be other than that he was expanding his position in the organization. Since, like so many Palestinians, he idolized Ghani Irabi, he couldn't bring himself to open the letter since it was too personal and he sensed it was of no importance politically."

Leron liked Ali but, in view of the fact that he hadn't told him about the letter, the slender thread of trust between Ali and the Mossad was broken by this deception. However, Ali still had possible usefulness and Leron and his superiors felt that this was not a good time to confront him.

Leron was an explosives expert. After hearing the proposed mission he had doubts about whether or not Marielle could carry it out. It is one thing to want to be a hero, but to know you are going to your death in the performance of your mission is something that requires a mindset not usually found in the Western psyche. A spoiled American princess like Marielle Bennett was not a credible candidate for such a mission. She would have to be trained, and even if she were able to carry it off, getting the weapon into place would be nearly impossible. Leron was skeptical but tried to stay open-minded.

It had been the Israelis who provided the initial intelligence about Ghani's complex deep in the Yemen desert. They had several moles planted in the midst of these fanatics as it was built, but one by one they disappeared without a trace before they could reveal its location. The Israelis believed there must be a deep cover agent operating at the CIA because their agents began to disappear after the American government was first briefed.

Leron felt a small nuclear device should be used. "Get the rats in their nest," he suggested.

Marielle felt otherwise. She was against a nuclear device. As she put it, "You don't use an elephant gun on mice. There is no need to rip a hole the size of the Grand Canyon to destroy the place. Morty's fuel-cell-and-plastique bomb will do what needs to be done quite handily.

"In addition, you don't know what they've got in their arsenal. The Russians are missing several suitcase bombs and the Chinese have been selling God knows what to whom. Morty's work was most promising and non-polluting, and would no doubt have eventually replaced nuclear if the Cold War continued."

Marielle clearly knew what she was talking about. This further irked Leron, who wondered silently, *What if she gets it on with Irabi and decides to switch sides.* He had so many misgivings about this affair he felt like walking out the door. He knew the drill, however, and he didn't want to get kicked upstairs for not cooperating with the CIA. Like every Israeli, he knew where his bread was buttered.

Marielle spoke again, and to Leron's further chagrin, she made more sense than either of the two generals from the Joint Chiefs or the DOD scientists.

She told them, "When Morty conducted tests for the Atomic Energy Commission, they found you didn't need the same amount of bang to get your buck's worth underground, so a small device using the combination of fuel cells and plastique should suffice. And it would look like an accident. No need to have more fury and anger dropped on the doorstep of the U.S."

Leron couldn't help respecting her input, but his mistrust and anger over how she made a fool of him so many years ago overshadowed everything. He was a man who had little use for women. His mother had made him a bit of a mama's boy, and since he was able to go out on his own, she had warned him of the wicked ways of women. His father, a survivor of Auschwitz, was obsessed with giving his all to the Jewish state and proudly raised his only son to serve that dream. Israel and her needs came above all else. Leron was there to observe and guide. Those were his orders and they came directly from Sharon.

The plans presented that afternoon at Langley were the stuff sci-fi is made of. Even the process for the making of the kind of radioactive material they needed was in the experimental stage.

Marielle would actually leave her life behind and move, lock, stock, and barrel, to the Middle East. She'd send her personal belongings to London and then to the United Arab Emirates. From there, she'd expect Ghani to have her things delivered to wherever they would live, most likely the complex in Yemen.

The bomb would be inside the movement of the heirloom grandfather clock that Ghani would remember from the foyer of her Oyster Bay mansion. The explosive material would be created and concealed in the experimental plastic shield with electronic diodes to confuse any sophisticated detectors.

Marielle would carry the trigger in the form of a makeup compact, also masked with this stealth material. It would work in combination with a panel underneath the clock. Either she would set it from the panel or use the trigger as long she was in range. The compact trigger would cause an immediate detonation while the panel would give her thirty minutes' time, something she specifically requested so she could confront Ghani with what she was doing. She needed this closure.

She would settle in for a few weeks, and by the time her furniture and belongings arrived, she would be ready to carry out the mission.

Marielle knew the clock was running and at stake was the survival of the Western world. The extensive news coverage had made it plain that the plans these fanatics had in the works, if successful, would wreak horrible acts of terror all over the world. Without the guidance of this evil mastermind and his senior henchmen the various worldwide Islamic terrorist organizations would be without funds or leadership. This seemed to be the only chance to stop these people dead in their tracks.

Chapter Eleven

MARIELLE WROTE A CAREFULLY THOUGHT-OUT LETTER to Ghani. It read:

Dearest Ghani,

When last we saw each other, I began counting the minutes until I would see you again. As the minutes turned into weeks, the weeks into months, the months into years, I began to accept the fact that you would not be sending for me. That I would never see you again. That my dreams of a life with you were simply the dreams of a silly lovesick girl. How many times I cursed you for not at least contacting me, for not letting me know how you were, for not caring how I was. I tried my best to forget you.

Now, thirty-two long years later, at my time of deep sorrow you ask to come back into my life. And as much as I would like to be strong enough to say no, I realize that I never stopped loving you. Now, after learning how fragile life can be, I understand that to be given this second chance for happiness is more precious than gold.

I will come to you whenever and wherever you wish. If it is possible, I'd like to bring a few of my most cherished possessions. I guess they could be sent to London for storage until you can arrange to get them and have them sent to where we will make our home.

I know you will understand I need some of my personal things to make me comfortable. I will not sleep until I am in your arms again.

My love, you are my destiny.

Your true love,
Marielle

After writing the letter, she contacted June Winters and asked her to make sure that it got into Ghani's hands. She gave the letter to her and thanked her for being the angel who made it possible for her to be reunited with Ghani.

Now that the wheels had been placed in motion, there was no turning back. What would she tell Caroline? After John Paul's death, she and Caroline had begun to develop a much closer relationship. Now suddenly that would come to an end. What she told Caroline was only half-truth for she did still truly love Ghani. What she decided not to share was that in spite of her intense feelings for him, she was obsessed with the need to right the wrong he perpetrated on mankind with his misguided and fanatical efforts to destroy the West. Marielle did not tell Caroline of her true mission. She didn't want to burden her daughter with that knowledge.

Caroline was stunned and sickened to hear of her mother's plans to reunite with the man who nearly destroyed her family. She was furious at how, once again her mother was letting him interfere in their life. Marielle stared at her daughter's growing belly, knowing she'd never see her grandchild. *I'm doing this for all the grandchildren, everyone's grandchildren. I alone can stop this man and I will,* she thought.

"Mother, I just wish you would reconsider," Caroline pleaded. "Going half way around the world to pick up with an old lover whom you haven't seen in thirty years is insane. What kind of a character is he? Mother, you're a wealthy and vulnerable woman. Think about it. It's not even romantic; it's nuts and dangerous, besides everything else."

"I have to see him. He never knew about our John Paul. He has a right to know he had a son. Caroline, you have a husband and a new baby coming. Your life is full. You'll go back and settle in with Patrick in London. The new baby will keep you busy and I will be all alone now. I'm in limbo. Please understand. I need to find closure. I have to find happiness with the man I've never stopped loving. You need to let me go."

"Mother I know you can and will do whatever you want, but I don't know if I will, if I can ever forgive you," Caroline screamed.

The next ten days were busy ones. Marielle packed her things and arranged to have them sent to London. She had not yet heard back from Ghani but she assumed she would be able to talk him into bringing along her things. If he loved her then he would understand.

The CIA made plans for her to go for special training to prepare for her mission. She would be trained in a crash course in the martial arts as well as the handling of sensitive explosives. She told both Caroline and June she was going on a spiritual retreat to prepare herself for her new life. Both believed her. Her religious convictions were evident to all who knew her. She always wore the large gold and diamond cross her mother gave her, even in the shower. Before she could leave she wanted to dismantle John Paul's apartment. Neither Marielle nor Caroline felt comfortable about it, but as Marielle pointed out to her daughter, "Some things are inescapable and this sad task is one of them."

Caroline asked Lily Wentworth if she wanted to help decide what to do with Susan's belongings; most specifically her diary, which was locked. Although Caroline found its key she didn't feel right opening it.

It seemed like only yesterday that they interred the lovers and the pain of their mutual loss was still fresh like a hard-to-heal wound.

The apartment was sunny and wonderfully livable. The shelves were filled with a number of leather-bound, antique, first-edition books.

"Susan collected them since her teens," Lily told them. "Perhaps I should donate them to Foxcroft. She started collecting them her first year away at boarding school." Her eyes suddenly filled with tears. "You'll both have to excuse me," she said as she started to weep openly. "I don't think I can do this."

"Sit down," Marielle said gently. "Caroline, why don't you make us all a cup of tea. Tea helps just about everything. We can't bring them back but we can keep their memory alive in our hearts. We can make sure all their treasures are given to people who will make use of them."

As Caroline went about making tea, Marielle opened the bureau drawer and held one of John Paul's sweaters to her breast. She could not get the image of the horror of 9/11 out of her mind. Now it overwhelmed her.

"Mother, you look so pale. Are you all right?"

"Yes, honey, just caught up in my own thoughts," she replied pensively.

"Here's your tea. Sit down," Caroline said as she handed Lily hers and went over to get her own.

The kitchen window had been converted into a mini greenhouse planter that was now filled with dead orchids. How lovely they must have been when they were in full bloom.

Lily remarked how Susan and John Paul shared her love of gardening.

"You know, my orchids were judged best in the show last year at the Garden Club party at Coe Hill. Susan and John Paul came to the event. They were so in love. I wish you could've seen them together. It comforts me to know how happy they were."

Marielle couldn't accept the fact that her son kept his relationship with Susan from her. She got up, completely ignored what Lily was saying, and began to empty the closet.

Caroline touched Lily's arm and said, "I'm happy too that my brother was lucky enough to find love before he died."

Marielle neatly separated John Paul's clothes from Susan's. "Caroline, you and Lily can put these things into the boxes I had delivered. We'll label them and then arrange for the Salvation Army to come and get them."

"Marielle," Lily said, hesitating. "I'd prefer Susan's things to go to Housing Works. It's a wonderful organization that helps people living with AIDS."

Marielle, realizing she was taking too much control of the situation, said, "Why that's fine Lily. Whatever you prefer is all right with me."

"Well, there's enough here," Caroline added, "to give to both organizations."

The idea of her brother's things going anywhere made her sad and the queasy feeling of morning sickness bothered her even though it was early afternoon.

Marielle wanted to keep her son's desk. She gave it to him right after college and it was the only thing he took with him when he moved out. She remembered him saying he wanted everything new but he couldn't get along without his desk. She pictured him sitting at it.

"I'm going to put it right back in John Paul's sitting room," she said. "Right where it was."

Now everything will be the same as before he moved out, Caroline thought. Her mother hadn't touched anything on that floor. She had laughed then behind her mother's back, thinking that it was like some kind of ridiculous shrine. Her thoughts almost haunted her now for when the desk returned it would be a shrine.

Marielle took a few select articles of clothing and was putting them aside in a large Bergdorf Goodman shopping bag.

Lily noticed and she caught Caroline's eye. Neither woman said a word.

Marielle saw their look. "Listen, I'm holding onto whatever I can. There are some things I'll probably never be ready to part with."

"Believe me," Lily said. "I understand perfectly. I'm not ready to open Susan's diary and maybe I'll never be. I plan to take it home and put in her old room." She started to cry again as she picked up the book, her fingers caressing the gold clasp.

"Could I please have the key?" she asked.

"Of course," Caroline said as she opened the drawer and handed it to Lily.

"I'm going to go home now," Lily said. "I don't feel very well, frankly, and I want to be alone."

"Of course," Marielle said. "Caroline and I will finish this up."

"Thank you," Lily said. "I don't know where you get your strength but I admire you so for it."

After Lily left, Caroline put her arm around her mother.

"Mother you are a rock in so many ways but if you need to just let it all go I'm here for you."

"Darling, I'm really looking forward to the retreat. I'll be able to reconcile things better once I've had a rest and been able to pray."

It was arranged that the Assumption of Mary Convent in Biddeford, Maine, would receive telephone calls for her, which would be transferred by satellite to CIA training headquarters in Langley. Training Marielle in such a short time would have been unrealistic except that she was extremely athletic, an expert skier and horse-woman who, until recently, worked out daily, and could bench press 150 pounds. She often went on wilderness trips with John Paul, and together they did a bit of mountain climbing. She could run circles around people half her age. She was to be trained by four special ops experts and Red Connors, a legend within the spy community.

The special ops training camp was tucked into a thirty-four-acre tract in the West Virginia hills. It looked like a private school complete with a sign that read, "Gable Down Institute." There was pretty shrubbery surrounding the brick pillars of the entrance that framed the white board fencing that seemed to go on for miles. Red Connors was there to greet her. Marielle hadn't the faintest idea what two weeks spent there would be like but took her mission very seriously.

"Let's get you settled first," he stated as he took her bags. "Then I'll show you around. You'll be staying up here in the main house." Red was very direct with Marielle. "I'll be responsible for getting you ready for just about anything you'll encounter over there. What I'm going to teach you here will be the only thing standing between you and death. So listen up, girlie. Pay close attention because you won't get second chances in the field. We'll be cramming six weeks of intensive training into two. It won't be easy."

Marielle cut him off. "I'm up for it whatever it is," she said, staring at him earnestly.

"Yes, ma'am, I believe you are. Why don't you unpack?" he suggested.

"No, that's okay. I'll unpack later. I'd like to see the place."

"Your call, ma'am."

As they drove down the dirt road in a camouflaged Hummer, Marielle wondered just what she'd be doing here to prepare. She didn't have to wait long as they rounded a corner. She was surprised that they were in fact on a military base. They approached a gate, which was protected by marines with assault rifles. The fence was at least 35 feet high and had barbed wire at the top. She wondered if it was there to keep you out or in. It was intimidating.

"What are you thinking?" Red asked. "Perhaps you're having second thoughts?"

"Oh, no," she said smiling. "No second thoughts."

"Look," Red said. "I'd like to think when your training here is completed you will understand just what you're getting into. Then if you still think you are capable of this kind of hellish work, so be it."

"Red," she teased, "just what is so hard or how smart do you have to be to set and press a bomb trigger? It's a no-brainer."

"All the same and with all due respect, ma'am, humor us and let us at least do what we can to ensure you have the skills one of us would have if we were assigned such a mission."

He parked the Hummer. "Come on, I want you to meet Master Chief Gooding," he said.

"Hey Red," the old warrior said, saluting his friend. "And welcome aboard our operation readiness exercises, ma'am. We've set up a few scenarios you might encounter on this mission. We'll do our best to make sure you'll be able to handle yourself. The fact that there'll be no exit plan in place for you is just tough for me to take. Your bravery is truly inspiring."

"Chief Gooding, when can I really get started?" she asked.

"Right now if you'd like. The first order of business is to build you up, get you fighting fit." He grinned. "I hope you like to run, ma'am."

"I sure do," she said, smiling.

"Then let's get you some gear and you can train with a couple of CIA gals who are being deployed to Afghanistan." Marielle couldn't believe how rough and uncomfortable the army sweats were. *Ugh,* she thought as she dressed. *Why do I need to wear these?*

"Red," the master chief said while Marielle was gone, "are they getting nutsy at the company or what? We're now training split-tail socialites to go on suicide missions to deliver up targets our guys can't even find?"

"Look, Goodie, I don't dream up the ops. I just try to make them work. Don't underestimate her."

"Bullshit, after a couple of days here, she'll fold. No civilian is going to stand up to the punishment. Hell, Red, even some of the guys Langley sends over here end up in a pile of tears."

Marielle struggled a little with the weight of her backpack when she joined the others. Most of these women were officers from the army and navy, and one marine, who'd been assigned to the CIA to be trained for active duty. They were young, mean, lean, and less than enthusiastic about training with this person their mothers' age. In addition, they had no idea why she was there and never would.

The marine, a husky girl named Nancy Bass, asked Marielle if she was a reporter. Marielle just smiled not answering.

"Stand easy, ladies," the master chief said. "We'll start slow. Two miles this morning." He drove alongside them as they jogged down the trail.

Marielle loved running and finished the New York Marathon about eight years ago. But the weight of the backpack and the bulky clothing and heavy boots made it really hard for her to keep up. After running about three-quarters of a mile, she began to feel real pain in her lower legs and back.

Chief Gooding drove up alongside her. "Ready to say uncle, ma'am?" he taunted.

"Hell no," she shouted back defiantly. She told herself to keep putting one foot in front of the other. Two miles is not that far. She put her mind on John Paul. *This is for you, son. This is for you,* she thought.

Before she knew it, it was over. She did it. She didn't give up. She had an awful pain in her side but it would go away soon enough and to her surprise the women half her age were spent, too.

They began at dawn every day, rain or shine, and went through exercises similar to actual combat conditions. She ran until she fell down. She crawled through waist-high mud. She shivered half-dressed as a pseudo-terrorist browbeat her with endless questions. She learned how to lie well enough to pass a lie detector test. She also learned just how to make, arm, and disarm a bomb. She was bruised and sore from endless karate sessions.

"You never know when you will be discovered and need to defend yourself," Red said, over and over.

She laughed as they insisted on building up her ability to withstand combat. "This is a one-way trip for me. Anyway, it's my Mata Hari skills we have to worry about."

She dreamed of her daughter and the grandchild to come. She spoke to both Caroline and June regularly. "I'm praying," she would say. "It's so peaceful here. I walk with the sisters and try to be as serene as they are." God, her lying was even starting to convince her.

She hated lying all her life and now, to become truly expert at it was kind of funny in a sick sort of way. Goodie was on her case twenty-four hours a day. He berated her relentlessly. She didn't arm a bomb correctly and in a real situation would have blown herself up before it was supposed to go off. He never let her forget that. Marielle was scared she might not be able to carry out her end, but never let on about her doubts to anyone but herself.

She did more soul searching during those two weeks than she had ever done in her life. Convinced she was as ready as she would ever be, she asked Red to throw everything he had at her.

"Little lady," Red said, "I don't think so." He laughed. "I want you to leave here in one piece so you can at least attempt this mission impossible. Get it? Impossible mission. Only there won't be any Tom Cruise over there to save you."

Red was particularly interested in what would make a rich, powerful woman willing to sacrifice her life like this. Marielle tried to explain herself.

"Red, you know I am partly responsible for what happened to my country by a silly romantic and foolish thing I did years ago when I helped Ghani Irabi escape his fate. You also know I have paid for this with my child's life. I need to stop him before he can hurt anyone else. I am the one person who can stop this evil man. Don't you see? I really have no choice. If someone doesn't stop him, he will set the whole world on fire with his hatred."

"I guess you must really despise him," Red said.

"I don't know, Red. I loved him once and I wish things had been different. I never truly knew him, I guess. I loved a person who didn't really exist outside my own mind. I know what must be done now, and in spite of the fact that he was the love of my life, I will kill him."

Red had never met a woman like her, and he'd known many women. She was the best candidate of any age they had turned out. She was now as deadly an assassin as any experienced field agent. She was surprisingly adept at working with explosives, and she was now capable of both arming and disarming highly sophisticated bombs. Red had no doubt she was ready, but he was concerned about what she was up against; people feared even by the Mossad. He wished there was some other way.

Her fellow trainees began to have a deep respect for the woman they called "Mrs. Mystery." They had been in camp for over a month when she'd joined them in training. It was impressive that she had the second highest scores now, even in hand-to-hand combat.

"The lifeline of a combat unit is the teamwork," Red said. "Even though you'll be pretty much alone over there, the Israelis are trying to find a way to get an agent inside to help back you up."

"It's pretty lame to send someone in just to get killed," Marielle remarked. "This is a one-man job," she laughed. "I mean person, Red." He laughed, too.

The two weeks flew by and she felt more confident that she'd successfully take Ghani and his cohorts to their day of reckoning. The night before her return to New York they gave a party for her. She made friends here as she did wherever her life took her.

In the morning just before they left she told Master Chief Gooding that she hated to leave her "greens" behind, referring to her military outfit and gear.

"Good luck and God speed, Ma'am," he said choking up with emotion.

Red opened the car door and she got in.

There was one more briefing before Marielle returned to New York to await Ghani's instructions. Several high-level CIA operatives and Leron Yitzaki of the Mossad were present. Leron was a volatile man and couldn't help but confront Marielle for what she did thirty-two years before.

"You are a traitor," he said. "You are scum to have saved a monster like Hitler." Leron was clearly out of control. He slapped her across the face. Marielle, acting on impulse, and using her new skills, jumped against him, crushing his chest with her feet and slamming him with her small fist. Leron didn't see it coming and was out cold on the floor. Red raised his eyebrows and smiled.

"Jeez, Louise. I was worried about you, little darling," he said. "But I guess you can take care of yourself. One Mossad black belt down ain't bad for a day's work."

Marielle hugged him. "Thank you for all you've taught me," she said. "I'll do you all proud, I promise. I'm really good at this stuff, you know."

Her little-girl sweetness, still so much a part of her, touched even the hardest heart. They all wished her well. So much depended on what she was going to do.

She slept on the plane that took her to Biddeford, Maine. She'd fly home from there. She marveled at the intelligence community's attention to detail.

Chapter Twelve

MARIELLE GOT BACK TO HER NEW YORK TOWNHOUSE very late. She went right to bed and fell asleep the second her head hit the soft down pillow. In the morning she began to go through her mail and listen to her phone messages. Caroline came over for breakfast. "I hope the retreat helped you come to your senses, Mummy."

"Caroline, dear, I need to follow my heart just this once in my life. I love you so much more than you realize. Don't worry. You'll come to see me, or I'll meet you and Patrick in London after the baby is born," she said, trying to sound sincere.

Caroline was bitter. She hoped her mother would be with her for the birth. Marielle wanted to explain to Caroline, but she knew she couldn't tell her the truth. Caroline was not even angry; just disappointed and once again feeling abandoned.

"Well, Mother, I've got to go to the obstetrician this morning so I'll be on my way. I'll stop over later. Will you be home?" She hoped her mother would offer to go along so she'd be able to see her grandchild on the sonogram machine, but as always she was too busy. Had it been John Paul's child surely she'd have been at his wife's side. Holding her hand no doubt.

"Yes," Marielle said. "I've got a lot of paperwork and bills to pay. I'll see you later, dear."

After Caroline left, Marielle sat down to write a letter to be opened only upon her death. She couldn't find the right words to explain what she was about to do. Then the phone rang. It was June.

"Marielle, I have something for you. May I come over tomorrow?"

"Yes," she answered. "I'll be watching for you. About what time will you be here?"

"Around eleven or so," June said.

Marielle hung up the phone, knowing her fate was sealed. Yet she was unafraid. To be truthful, she was excited. *One can never appreciate life as much as when one is about to lose it,* she thought. *It's not how long you live; it's how you live and what you do with your life.* She desperately wanted to spare the world another 9/11, and she was going to do just that.

June arrived at 11:15 the following morning. It was the 30th of November. It was unusual for June, who was such a hard worker, to take a day off, Marielle thought.

"Marielle, I have your itinerary. You—I mean *we*—are leaving next Sunday for Dubai. My brother says I'm to accompany you to make sure you are safe. I'm also going to teach you about the customs of Islam. Once you are over there, you will have to cover yourself. You will not be made to wear the burka, but you will wear the chador in public places. Here are the papers for you and also the information about the storage facility in London where your furniture and trunks will be sent.

"I am so excited about seeing Ali again. I've taken a six-week leave of absence from my job at Lenox Hill. I am also going to be trained so I can play a greater role in our goal of Islamic rule over Jerusalem, and the end of Israel. For that to happen we must bring the Great Satan, America, to its knees," she said, seriously.

June was given to outbursts, and the more she knew of June the more Marielle thought she was unstable. Marielle couldn't stand to even think there was a possibility of such a thing happening and it furthered her resolve to carry out her mission and destroy these sick and misguided fanatics once and for all. She didn't have it in her to hate anyone. She had always believed in the goodness of all people, but after what had happened on 9/11 she realized that sometimes, in order to save the good and innocent, evildoers must be savagely destroyed.

Marielle felt sorry for June. June was really a nice person deep down, but her mind had been shaped by a childhood surrounded by warlike conditions in Lebanon and then an abusive adoptive home. Her childhood memories of horror caused her to live a life of hatred and vengeance seeking.

Normally, Marielle would have no feelings of revenge. She was a true American. She loved her fellow man and cared about the world. She felt somewhat like a doctor and imagined herself ready to cut away a cancer in order to allow a body to live. These fanatics were cancers on the world's body, and it was a proper and justifiable cause to be part of their removal.

June saw Marielle was deep in thought, so she quietly sat down and waited for her to finish looking over the papers she brought to her. Finally she said, "Marielle, can you begin to understand the plight of our people, born into fear and humiliation at the hands of the Israeli Zionists? We are hungry not only for food and a decent life, but also for our dignity. These Zionists take away everything. We have nothing but our determination to free our homeland from these interlopers, and we are willing to give our lives in that effort. We have our lives to give, and we give them gladly. As the flesh of our martyrs is blown from their bones, we glorify that moment when they sacrifice everything for our cause.

"I remember my mother and father the day the Israeli soldiers killed them in cold blood. They hid me under an old refrigerator, and told me not to come out no matter what. My father told me to be brave and perhaps someday all the blood our people have paid in this struggle will pay for the return of our homeland.

"Hearing the rocket fire and the buildings crumbling I cowered in the darkness in fear. I would never see him again, or my mother. They were both killed during that fierce fighting. Death to Israel!" June ranted in an almost trancelike state.

Marielle recoiled at June's diatribe. Her Jekyl and Hyde personality was startling and disturbing. Marielle wondered if she suffered from a personality disorder. She could almost seem delusional at times, but at this point she needed to appease her as part of the CIA plan.

Marielle just wanted June to go away and leave her alone. She needed to be alone now. June was a fanatic, and nothing she could say would change that.

"June," Marielle finally said. "I have so many things to do before we leave next Sunday. You'll just have to excuse me now. We'll speak during the week, and of course we'll go together to the airport Sunday afternoon." She embraced her and let her out.

As she closed the door she went back to her desk. *Now is as good a time as any,* she thought, *to write that letter to Caroline.*

But try as she might, she just couldn't seem to make sense. After crumpling half a dozen pieces of stationery she finally set forth the thoughts she only wanted her sweet girl to know after she was gone. She must get this done, and now. *Rise to the occasion,* she commanded herself as she put her pen to the paper.

My Dearest Caroline,

How hard it is for me to leave you. Even harder to know that you think I am running to the happiness of a lover's arms. Life can be so complex, my sweet little girl. I was very confused those many years ago when I

130

let my emotions and love for a man not your father put my entire family in harm's way. I was young, foolish and passionate, and my reckless behavior almost cost me my family.

It was only the goodness and forgiveness of your father, God rest his soul, that saved me and the baby I was carrying. You thought I didn't love you as much as I did John Paul, but Caroline I loved you just as much. Don't ever doubt it. I was protective toward John Paul because I was afraid people would reject him, and if it had not been for your father, who was a living saint, they would have. He alone made it clear to one and all that he'd tolerate nothing if it were to hurt either of his children. I am so sorry for how you've suffered because of me.

I hope you will understand now just why it appears I am turning my back on you and, indeed, even my country. I am trying to right the old wrongs and while I may never be able to make up to you for the deceit, I will be doing something necessary, and important, that will make the world safer for you and Patrick and the beautiful new baby I will, sadly, never see.

I know that Ghani Irabi was responsible for the vicious attack on the World Trade Center and for John Paul's death, as well as other acts of despicable terror. I am not going to him out of love, although I love the man I thought he was, and could have been, had he not been twisted into a monster by his fanatical and hateful beliefs.

I am going to destroy him. I am the only person on earth whom he trusts enough to get close enough to successfully defeat him. I will be making a sacrifice to do this, and I want you to understand and be proud of what I am going to do.

I will always be with you in my heart, sweet Caroline, and with my death will pay for my foolish act thirty-two years ago, when I saved his life and enabled him to wreak his havoc and hatred on the world.

I am sorry, sweet angel, to have to deceive you one last time. Forgive me and celebrate me. I have always loved you and always will.

Your loving Mother,
Marielle

She brushed aside her tears as she put the letter into an envelope and sealed it. She wrote on the front: *To be opened only in the event of my death.* Then she put it in her personal briefcase with 20,000 shares of IBM, 10,000 shares of General Motors Corp., and $350,000 in cash. She signed the backs of the certificates and left another envelope marked "To my grandchild 'Baby Larson.'"

As she placed the note inside the envelope she decided to reread it.

Sweet child of my heart,

I have pictured you in my mind a thousand times. Are you a bundle of pink joy or are you a blue boy? Whatever you are you will bring happiness to your sweet mother, my baby girl who I love so much.

I won't ever meet you, but I will be a part of your life. You will be proud of me, your old grandma, and I will know you as I watch you grow from somewhere beyond the heavens, from behind the rainbow.

*Take care of your mother for me and know how much
I love you.*

Grandma Marielle

Marielle left the numbers of her life insurance policy and the bro-
kerage account that she and Dr. Bennett shared in the top drawer of
her desk with the two letters. Even in this God-awful market, the
account was worth more than $72 million, and their several money
market and bank accounts had in excess of another $30 million. She
transferred $5.5 million to a newly opened account in Switzerland
for her personal use over the next several weeks or months, until she
would no longer need it.

During the week before Marielle was scheduled to leave, she
saw very little of her precious Caroline, who was completely disgusted by what her mother was going to do, and just couldn't deal
with it.

Finally, Saturday, Caroline and Patrick came by. Marielle had
everything ready to give them, explaining she was leaving the bulk
of her holdings in the States, to be managed by Morgan Stanley, except her personal shares that she had always held herself. These
shares, plus $350,000 in cash, were there for Caroline to watch over.
Her important jewelry would stay in the vault at Citibank. She was
only taking a few pieces with her.

Caroline had a hard time hiding her feelings, and it was obvious
that Patrick was just completely at the end of his tether. He told
Marielle he was shocked she could do this to her family. He even
suggested to Caroline they temporarily commit her for psychiatric
testing, but Caroline said absolutely not. That would make the press
for sure. "No one knows about this, thank God, except us, so there
will be no scandal. Mother is just having a hard time getting over

her grief." Caroline hoped she'd quickly tire of her life with that "sand nigger."

Caroline told Marielle she thought it best if she and Patrick didn't go to the airport with her tomorrow afternoon. "I'd like to say goodbye tonight, Mother." Marielle's heart ached, and she couldn't hold back her tears. Caroline was crying now, too. Marielle hugged her and bent over to kiss her belly. Patrick walked out without saying a word. Marielle thought, *How very British of him.* She held on to Caroline and wept. She said, "Don't worry. Your life is going to be wonderful. Patrick loves you. You are beautiful. You're going to be a mother yourself. Your life is a book of empty pages, which will be written on and molded by you. My life is etched in the past. I can only go forward if I go back to what I lost. I want to try to find what I lost. Please understand, I need to do this. Please don't judge me. Believe in me, and know that no matter where I am I am always your mother."

"Mother, I feel there's something you're not telling me."

"There are some things we have no words for, sweet child." They said goodbye, and Caroline was gone.

Marielle sank to the floor, and in her grief she allowed herself to sob loudly. This would be the last time she'd be free to express any real emotion. Her mistakes as a mother swirled in her head. How she wished she had it to do all over again. She would have done things so differently. Funny how Monday morning quarterbacking lets you see so clearly how things should have been. *Alas, it's too late, and why beat yourself up over something that's totally beyond your control, gone with the Champagne wishes and caviar dreams.* She laughed to herself. *Who would even believe my life. No one could make up stuff like this.*

She was sorry for her lost opportunity to be the model parent her children deserved. John Paul was gone and there was no time left to make it up to Caroline and the grandchild she'd never see. Her tears streamed down in a river of pain and regret.

Cry your eyes out. Forget what could have been; just deal with what is and what must be done. She tucked a baby picture of Caroline and John Paul into her carry-on bag and snapped it shut.

Marielle could not get to sleep, no matter how hard she tried. She thought of her father and how she had loved him, wishing he had lived to see Caroline and John Paul. She wondered again if her father suffered as the car crashed and he was crushed by the glass and engine into his seat. An awful death, to say the least.

Her mother Elizabeth had been so strict with her, not allowing her to date and sending her off to an all-girls college. It was no wonder she married Morty. He was the first and only man in her life until Ghani swept her off her feet.

She found herself wishing things had been different. She'd have grown up and married someone her own age and never met Ghani. She'd just have lived an average life and had an average family. *If I keep thinking about this, I'll go stark, raving mad,* she thought.

The image of her mother lying so peacefully on the satin pillow of the bronze casket suddenly made her realize she hadn't ever really known her mother. One moment she had been alive and vital and in a few hours a massive heart attack had ended it all. She dismissed Elizabeth as just a shallow, aging rich girl, but perhaps in reality her mother had been devastated by her father's blatant philandering, and then his horrific death and had hidden her heartbreak by staying on the endless, empty merry-go-round that the Boston social whirl can be.

Now she was thinking of her own death. Would she be brave, knowing her body would be blown into pieces and her flesh torn from her bones? She trembled at the thought, but was firm in her resolve. *Don't think about it until you must,* she ordered herself. *Enjoy the time you have left; live in the moment. Pretend everything is all right. Surely God will get you through this. You are a soldier in the army of God.*

She realized at once that she herself was not much different from an Islamic martyr except that she hoped her act would prevent more violence, not beget it. The senselessness of violence was clear to her, yet what must be done must be done. There would be no turning back after tomorrow. She thought of calling the whole thing off. As Leron had said, this was madness. Yet she knew she could no more call off her mission than stop a speeding train by standing before it with a match to flag it down.

No, the mission had grown bigger than everything. It would crush terrorist organizations and save millions of lives if, indeed, they were truly preparing to use on the West all means of terrorism, including biological warfare and possibly weapons of mass destruction.

Marielle got out of bed. She turned on the stereo and played the album she liked where Lee Greenwood sings, "I'm Proud to be an American for at least I know I'm free." She sang along with the CD. It made her feel good. How she wished she'd just feel tired, and now in addition to everything else she was hungry.

She headed for the kitchen and took a box of Famous Amos cookies out of the cupboard. She poured herself a large glass of milk and put an ice cube in it. She loved really cold milk with cookies. Somehow they always did the trick. She felt calm and a little sleepy now.

She looked at the clock. It was 2:45 AM. As she crawled under her covers, she began to drift off into sleep. When she awakened it was almost 10:00 AM. June would be there around noon, so she got up and began to get dressed.

Caroline called to wish her a safe flight and reminded her to e-mail as soon as she landed.

"If you change your mind for any reason, Mummy, just leave everything and come home," Caroline said, reassuringly.

"Don't worry, sweetheart. Everything will be fine. You'll see. We'll be together very soon, my precious." She felt awful lying to Caroline, but what else could she do? She couldn't tell her she was on her way to blow up Ghani and his world.

Chapter Thirteen

JUNE MET MARIELLE AT HER TOWNHOUSE WITH HER luggage. She rode into the city with Aziz Hamda, a member of one of Al Qaeda's sleeper cells in New York City. Aziz wanted to see Mrs. Bennett for himself. Even in the netherworld of these sick animals, gossip travels far and wide.

He happily carried June's bags into the courtyard of the beautiful townhouse. Marielle gave her housekeeper the weekend off, so she opened the door herself. Seeing June's two huge, overstuffed suitcases, Marielle thought it would take hours to go through airport security. She squeezed most of her clothes and accessory items such as extra cases of Q-Tips, soft toilet paper, shampoo and conditioner into several Louis Vuitton trunks. She also packed five cases of her favorite Mad River Iced Tea and Lemonade as well as cases of Coca Cola, which is next to impossible to get in the Middle East.

Ghani knew her as a woman who loved her creature comforts, so she knew he would think nothing of her being overpacked. In fact, he'd expect it. She wanted the last few weeks of her life to be as comfortable as possible. She wanted to avoid a long search at the airport, but *c'est la vie*! What's a couple of extra hours when you're off to save the free world? She would carry on one small Louis Vuitton suitcase, her Bergazin sable coat, and her makeup case. She had been careful to remove her tweezers and scissors and had packed them in other, checked bags.

Realizing Aziz was more than just a cab driver but was an obvious acquaintance of June's, Marielle asked him if he'd like to sit down. "Oh, no, madam," he said and abruptly left.

"Marielle, you must never ask a man, especially one you don't know, to sit down for a visit. You would surely be beaten for such an act. You must begin to understand Islam and a woman's place; otherwise you will prove an embarrassment to Ghani Irabi. Surely you would not want to embarrass so great a man as he."

"Surely not," said Marielle, trying to act sincere. "Dear June, thank God for you. You will teach me how to please my man."

June was more of a fanatic than Marielle could ever imagine. "Marielle," she said, "after my divorce, I wanted more than anything to return to my roots. I wanted to show Allah my total devotion to Islam. I had a female circumcision operation. It made me feel like I really belonged to my people. You know, there are a number of Islamic doctors right in the Tri-State Area who perform this surgery. It is very popular among my sisters. Marielle, you might want to consider making the sacrifice for Ghani. It's not so bad. It's done under anesthesia in the hospital not like the homeland where they do it to girls around twelve years of age with a razor blade. There is a greater danger for infection for a mature woman but I'm sure it could be arranged when we get there. I am so blessed Allah has chosen me to bring Ghani Irabi his soul mate."

Wide-eyed, Marielle was incredulous over June's fanaticism, the thought of such a procedure made her shudder but she let June think she was in full sympathy with her ideals. She was glad the CIA would take her into custody when she returned to New York and break up at least one sleeper cell. She couldn't imagine how she had ever allowed herself to feel sorry about betraying her. June was as bloodthirsty for murder and terror as bin Laden himself. She admonished herself for not having realized this earlier.

Marielle ordered a town car to take them to the airport. They were flying on British Airways, first class to London and then to Dubai. Someone named Hamsa was going to meet their plane. They were staying overnight at the Burj Al Arab Hotel where Ghani would meet them. They would enjoy a few days in Dubai and then, when her belongings arrived from London, they'd make their way to Yemen.

Once they were at the airport things went much more quickly than Marielle imagined. Going through security involved a painstaking piece-by-piece search of June's bags, and then a perfunctory search of Marielle's. While Marielle knew this was racial profiling, in view of what she personally knew of June, she realized that it was really necessary.

They were whisked off to the VIP lounge by a British Airways employee who asked Marielle if she was Lady Harlington's mum. "Yes," she said.

"Madam, I'm so sorry for the loss of your son. I read it in the paper. I'm surprised to see you're going to the Middle East."

Marielle smiled her radiant smile and said, "I'm going to try to help the orphans of that region. We must try to rebuild the world with love and understanding." The steward said nothing, but thought, *Just another rich asshole trying to save the world when we ought to be blowing those Arab bastards to hell.*

The flight was rather bumpy, and June talked incessantly about Islam and a woman's place and obligations. Marielle listened politely, but amused herself by thinking that even Allah would puke at having to listen to such trash. How could any woman believe this garbage? Maybe they have to submit to it because to refuse could mean being stoned to death. But to follow it freely and teach it to their daughters they must all have a screw loose.

"Yes June," she said every so often, or "uh huh." But her mind was again lost in her memories of her beloved John Paul, his life snuffed out like a candle so quickly, and for what?

She wondered over and over what his last moments had been like. Her son, her boy who never even knew the man who was really his father, the man she would kill, the man she once loved and maybe still loved. Marielle finally fell asleep and the flight attendant covered her with a blanket.

June woke Marielle gently. They would be landing in London in a few minutes. They were allowed to leave their belongings on the plane and disembark for half an hour or so if they wished, or they could remain on the plane. Marielle just wanted to sleep but June decided to get off for a while to stretch her legs.

When Marielle awoke again they had already taken off and were three hours into the flight. The film *America's Sweetheart* with Julia Roberts and Catherine Zeta-Jones was the in-flight movie. Marielle decided to watch it, but June did not, mumbling something to the effect that movies weren't permitted in Islam. She was turning into one scary bitch, Marielle thought.

What is allowed? Her face must have shown what she was thinking because June said, "Enjoy it, because there will be no more movies in your new life. You'll be too busy pleasing your husband."

"June, I know Ghani very well. He loves movies. He loves music and dancing. In fact, he's a marvelous dancer. I promise you he's not going to deny me anything that makes me happy." At once she was sorry she said anything at all. "Dear June," she said to the obviously ruffled woman, "I know you are trying to help teach me your way of life. Forgive me if I showed any disrespect. I'll try to understand better, but you don't know Ghani as I do and he is not the rigid man you think he is. I'm sure he can't have changed that much or he wouldn't have sent for me."

Marielle put her headphones back on and settled into her seat. The movie was hilarious and she lost herself in it.

Before long they were approaching the runway. The turquoise blue water of the Persian Gulf had an exquisite sort of beauty. Dubai was as cosmopolitan as Paris. Sheik Mohammed's racehorses were world famous. Marielle forced herself to think of happy things. That was the only way she could go through with this charade.

Her happiest thought was that she would soon be in Heaven with John Paul, watching from above as a guardian angel to Caroline and the new baby, but together again with her precious boy. He'd meet his father at last, and maybe Allah, God, or Jesus could forgive Ghani. She felt terribly sad suddenly, for she knew he would have to bear the punishment and wrath of God for what he'd done, and so would she.

Then she thought of Morty. He was such a good man. Unable to confront her, he accepted John Paul as his own and made their life together truly as a family. Marielle prepared herself for whatever was to come. She asked God to give her the strength she'd need to do what must be done and to forgive her, for she knew taking any life was against His holy commandments.

The plane landing was less than perfect as it blew a tire and they zigged and zagged all over the tarmac. Marielle wondered if it was an omen of some sort. But soon they were on the ground, safe for now.

As they deplaned, she noticed the military security. Young men not much more than eighteen or nineteen years old nervously clutched Kalashnikov assault rifles. She saw similar ones at Langley, though she was trained on Scorpion assault weapons. She could hear Red Connors repeating, "The magazine must be full in the well. Pull the slide back, squeeze the trigger, don't pull it. Let it fire." *My God, the power of those weapons,* Marielle thought. *They can cut a person in half in nanoseconds.*

She and June went through immigration security. They had to show their visas and letters of immigration. Marielle was surprised by the deference the officer showed after he saw their papers. The

Mercedes from the hotel waited outside. It was so warm Marielle knew at once that her coat was unnecessary. *Oh well,* she thought, *I really won't be needing it anymore anyway.* She smiled at the irony of everything and how things that were important to her once now meant nothing.

The driver took them to the hotel. Marielle was awed by the brilliant design and visual spectacle of the Burj Al Arab Hotel.

The desk clerk asked for their passports. "It is the custom, Madame, for us to hold our guests' passports during their stay with us." He was young and spoke perfect English. His beautiful dark eyes, with long eyelashes, reminded her of John Paul. Her mending heart was once again an open wound as she fought hard to hold back tears.

"Is anything wrong, madam?" he asked.

"No, no. It's just that you remind me of my son. He was killed recently and I still miss him so."

"I am sorry for your loss, madam," he replied. Then he rang for the bellman.

The 8,300-square-foot royal suite was over the top. Marielle had been in many luxury hotels, but this one was quite unforgettable— with red-and-gold-silk-lined walls and the intricate woodworking. The platform-framed king-size bed truly was the most beautiful and romantic place to sleep she had ever seen. June was aghast and said, "Allah would punish those who would dare create such wasteful opulence." Marielle just ignored her and began to unpack. She took off her shoes and was barefoot. June tried to get her to try on her chador. She also wanted her to remove her fingernail and toenail polish, and her makeup.

"June, we'll wait and see what Ghani wants. If he asks me to do these things, I will. But until he asks me, I will continue to do what is comfortable for me." She was getting annoyed, and was on the verge of losing her temper.

They didn't have to wait long as they soon heard the door of the suite opening. Marielle left the bedroom and entered the spacious and exquisitely furnished living room. There, in front of her, was Ghani, even more handsome than she remembered him. He looked elegant in an exquisitely tailored pin-striped suit. His salt-and-pepper hair was the only obvious physical change.

"My darling Marielle," he said as he moved quickly across the room until he was by her side. They embraced, and as he kissed her mouth, a flood of emotions raced through her body and mind. She still truly loved this man. *This misguided person of evil,* she thought, *is still very dear to me. How cruel fate is.* "The years have been so kind to you, I would have known you anywhere. I feel it was only yesterday when circumstances ripped us apart," he said passionately.

For both Marielle and Ghani the connection was immediate. The love they shared had been unconditional and even now transcended time and space. He picked her up in his arms and carried her into the bedroom. His bodyguards laughed like demented children, and she realized he was taking her like a piece of property. And while her own passions were on fire as well for want of this man, it would have made no difference to him. If she had been unwilling he'd certainly have raped her.

Tears flooded her eyes. Were they tears of joy for seeing him after all this time, or tears of sorrow for her fallen son? She didn't know. It wasn't that she didn't care. She did care. She was overcome with confusion just like a leaf caught in the rapids of a roaring river. She raised her eyes, looking deep into his, and was mesmerized by their beauty. Could he really be the architect of so much destruction? She knew the answer, but what did it really matter right now? What must be done would be done. She abandoned herself to him.

Marielle hated her body for it was consumed with desire for him. Her mind cried out for John Paul, but nothing would bring him back, she told herself. She felt alive for the first time in years.

Her love and hate for Ghani stirred inside her, so torn were her emotions as she felt him possess her.

Marielle was soon lost in the excitement of the moment. Her nails dug into his back as he took her over and over again. Then he kissed and licked her, pleasing her all over with his mouth and tongue. She climaxed repeatedly, screaming his name, until her body, exhausted and satisfied, floated in ecstasy. Her mind had shut down completely, and she fell asleep, nestled in the dark fur of his big, muscular chest.

In the morning he woke before her and ordered breakfast for both of them. He carried the tray into the room himself. It was obvious to her he was still madly in love with her.

"My dearest, your furniture and trunks arrived this morning. Do you want to open them and check for breakage yourself, or should my man check everything before it's handed on to our trucks for transport?"

He was trying to show Marielle respect by consulting her about her things. He had always been somewhat of a megalomaniac, and now, with his power at its acme, he looked upon her as his queen.

"Ghani," she replied, "we packed everything in yards of padding and bubble wrap. I'm certain it traveled well. However, for insurance purposes if anything was broken, have your men photograph it and send the pictures to the New York City moving company address on the boxes."

Ghani took her in his arms. "I've planned a lovely day for you. We'll go to the horse races, and then I've arranged for you to ride." He remembered how she loved horses and riding. Marielle had her boots and a pair of jodhpurs with her. She always took her riding clothes wherever she traveled in case the opportunity to ride presented itself.

He had a wonderful surprise for Marielle that morning. Smiling at her like a schoolboy with his first crush, he went into the bedroom and carried in several boxes, laying them on the bed. She was eating her lightly scrambled eggs and toast.

"Eat, darling, eat," he said. "I'll unwrap these gifts and show them to you."

First he unwrapped the largest package, giving her a description as he worked.

"For my beautiful Marielle from Chanel in Paris," he said. He pulled out an exquisite white suit and pale yellow blouse.

"Does it have long sleeves?" she inquired.

"Yes it does." He smiled. "Even Western women wear long sleeves in public in the Muslim world, my dear."

Next came the shoes and the matching handbag, custom made in white alligator from the artisan who created designs for Manolo Blahnik in Italy, and a little bag of lingerie.

"Ghani, how did you remember my size?" she exclaimed.

"That was not magic," he laughed. "We got the information from June Winters." Then he sat next to her on the bed, laying the breakfast tray on the floor. "I've saved the best for last," he said as he kissed her cheek. He reached into his pocket and brought forth a beautiful canary yellow diamond ring, surrounded by perfect D flawless diamonds.

"It's from Harry Winston," he proudly said as he slipped it on her left hand. "Do you like it?"

Marielle was touched by how considerate he was trying to be. The ring was beautiful and she loved it. For a moment she enjoyed the perfect exchange of love between two people. How tragic that they were star-crossed lovers, doomed by fate.

He held her now. "Marielle, I'm sorry for not sending for you as I promised to do so long ago. I have always loved you. I never married again and never had my own son, so I don't know how to comfort you in your loss. My wives live in Paris, and my daughters are married. I have three girl grandchildren, but no grandsons. If I have a regret, it is that I never had a son."

Marielle tenderly took his face in her hands. "Ghani, please believe what I am about to tell you," she said. "You had a son. My precious John Paul was your son. He was strong and good and loving and kind. He died because of hatred and evil and violence against those who are innocent. God took away our son, Ghani, because we sinned. Here, let me show you," she said as she took a tear-stained photo from her bag. "Pray for our son now with me."

Ghani was overcome with emotion as he saw himself in the boy. He stared at the photograph in utter disbelief. Could it be true? "I had a son and didn't know it? I, who have done so much to serve you, Allah, would be denied my son?" He raised his voice looking upward. "Why have you punished me so cruelly?"

"Ghani," Marielle said, "Remember how we used to pray together? We both knew God's holy commandments. In life, people pay for their sins and I have paid dearly for mine. Now all we have is each other."

Ghani started to shake, then wept. She tried to comfort him but nothing helped. He made a guttural sound that frightened her as he got up and walked away from her. He smashed his fist against the wall, cutting his hand and leaving a gaping hole. He collapsed sobbing on the floor, rocking back and forth. His bodyguards heard him cry out and burst into the room, their assault rifles pointing at Marielle.

"It's all right," she said.

Then Ghani, embarrassed by his own raw emotion, stood up. He looked coldly at her now.

"I will return in a few hours. Be ready to leave for the horse races at 1:30. We'll be lunching with Prince Naif."

As he turned and left she realized he had two separate personalities; the man she had loved, and still loved, and the cold, calculating monster who was the mastermind of the terrorist activities of every Muslim hate group known to man.

Chapter Fourteen

JUNE DIDN'T APPROVE OF THE GIFTS GHANI GAVE
Marielle, nor did she approve of the masseuse coming to the suite to
give Marielle a massage. In her mind, this was the very kind of deca-
dence she was fighting to rid the world of. It disgusted her even
more since it was happening in a Muslim country. How could their
supreme leader, Ghani Irabi, participate in this Western-style folly?
June left to take a long walk to gather her thoughts. She was disillusioned by the whole situation but chose to blame Marielle.

Marielle was relaxed that morning, even happy to some extent
although John Paul kept creeping into her thoughts. After the massage, she took a bubble bath. The tub was as big as a small swimming pool. She turned on the whirlpool and thought about what a
honeymoon people could have in this room. Then she remembered
John Paul and Susan decaying in the family tomb. Suddenly she felt
sick to her stomach. She got out of the tub, kneeled by the com-
mode, and lost her breakfast.

The ranges of up and down emotions were beginning to take a
toll on her. She cried again. *Get hold of yourself!* she heard her inner
voice say. *You can't afford the luxury of these kinds of emotions. Keep
yourself steady and focused.*

She sat at the vanity table and began applying her makeup. Then she put on the new Chanel suit. It fit perfectly. She looked quite lovely in it as she stood in front of the full-length mirror.

Ghani returned at 1:00 PM and by 1:30 they were off to the races. Sheik Mohammed bin Sultan al Nuhayyan spared no expense in the building of the facility. It was as elegant and well done as Churchill Downs. Billions of dollars had been spent in the Emirates to encourage the growth of flowers and lawns. Kentucky bluegrass had nothing on the green lawns of Dubai.

The races were exciting. Young Prince Naif joined them. Marielle wasn't sure if he was a Saudi or one of the sheik's relatives. She didn't feel it was proper to ask.

Ghani was so proud of her. He took her hand to show the prince her ring. Then he shocked her by telling the prince he just learned he and Marielle had a son whom he never knew. Smiling, he said his son died with the martyrs on 9/11.

"May Allah grant us more victories such as 9/11; many more in all the Western cities of the world," the prince replied.

"Soon," Ghani said. Marielle froze. These men were discussing mass murder and terrorist attacks as if they were talking about the weather. It was chilling to witness their exchange, but even more so to realize Ghani and his cohorts had the support of such powerful people—people who pretended to be friends of the United States.

"If only Mr. Abidi was still alive," the young prince said. "He was dedicated to our holy goals, and took great care of our monies until his bank was closed by the United States and Israel."

"They murdered him while his plane was taking him to seek medical treatment," Ghani said. "The Israeli agent who killed him was killed by our people in Iraq last year for trying to incite the Kurds."

Marielle acted as though she paid no attention, just watching the horses. She heard the prince ask Ghani if he planned to take her as a wife. He said, "Yes, I am going to honor Marielle and my fallen son by having a public wedding that will be attended by the heads of all our major supporters worldwide. The following week there will be attacks in every major Western city. We will have several days of celebration before the ceremony, and then, as we are joined as man and wife, blood will begin to run in the streets of the West."

Ghani turned to Marielle. "Don't worry about your precious Caroline. She and the family will be in Yemen for our wedding. They will be safe."

"Safe from what?" she said.

Ghani laughed and so did Prince Naif. "My woman would rather watch horses than listen to the talk of men."

"Unusual for a Western woman," the prince remarked.

After the last race, Ghani reminded her that he still had a surprise for her. They walked around to the stable area to see the horses. There was one particular grey stallion that caught her eye when he won the third race. He was beautiful but an Arabian, not a thoroughbred racehorse. He saw her look at him with admiration.

"Do you like that Arab horse, darling?"

"Yes, he's just beautiful," she said.

"He is yours, my love. When I knew you were joining me, I asked one of the Mujahadim officers if they had room for a horse for you in their stable within our complex. And while women are not normally allowed the privilege of a horse of their own, or, in fact, to ride, I have made you an 'honorary man.' The privilege will be yours. That's my surprise."

"Well, Ghani," she laughed, "I don't quite understand. What does that mean, 'honorary man'?" The idea seemed really silly to her but she tried to contain her mirth and waited for his explanation.

"Darling, it's kind of self-explanatory. In my world women keep their place," he said plainly.

"Exactly what does that mean?" she inquired coyly tilting her head to the side.

"Stop being flip about this, Marielle. It's different than when we were together in the States. An 'honorary man' has power. Women here have none. An honorary man can make decisions, a mere woman cannot. But don't get any ideas." He kissed her. "I want to be the master in my home." They both laughed, their eyes smiling.

"Want to be? I thought you were."

Marielle loved horses and owned them all her life. She was once again touched by the lengths to which he was extending himself to make her happy. *If only,* she thought, *he was not bent on wreaking havoc on the civilized world. Soon I will end this nightmare.* "Thank you, Ghani," she smiled. "Thank you my dearest."

Ghani's sexual appetite was like that of an eighteen-year-old boy. He was all over her again that night. He even suggested they try in-vitro fertilization. It had been done experimentally on a woman three years after menopause, he told her. He wanted another son.

At fifty-eight, Marielle had only recently begun menopause. Her periods were irregular. The thought of a change-of-life baby was more than she could bear. *Thank God we won't have to cross that bridge,* she thought. Although if things had worked out for them so long ago she'd have given him ten sons if he wanted them.

"Ghani, I brought something to show you. I was waiting for the right moment," she said as she got up and crossed the room. She opened her travel case and took out what appeared to be an old photo album.

How strange, she thought, *to talk about our son.* In truth, he didn't deserve to have any son after the carnage he caused on 9/11. She tried to hold in her anger and she forced a smile.

"Here, look at this one. He's taking his first steps and has fallen on his little butt. Here he is with his first pony, Doo Dah," she said pointing to another photo.

Ghani lovingly touched the yellowed photograph. "He is so like me isn't he?" he said proudly.

"That's true. No doubt he was your mirror image."

"Tell me about him."

"Just a handsome, charming, compassionate, socially conscious young man," she said biting her tongue.

"Why did you never tell him about me?"

"Ghani, he grew up in a different world. I had no idea where you were. It was for the best that he did not know the circumstances of his birth. People can be very unforgiving and it would have hurt him to know his mother was unfaithful to the only father he knew. Surely you can understand. I just couldn't tell him."

Ghani furrowed his brow deep in thought. He didn't reply.

Marielle continued, "Here look at him winning the soccer medal at Eaglebrook School. He was ten years old. So tall, don't you think? And look at him on skis all bundled up and ready for the slopes." She turned the page. "And this one with Caroline sailing in Hawaii, how he loved to sail. Why he and Morty restored an old sloop and sailed every Sunday during the summer on Long Island Sound."

"Was Morty a good father to my boy?" Ghani was a little unsure of himself.

"The best father a boy could have," she told him.

"A boy needs a father," Ghani said taking her hands in his. "I am grateful for his acceptance of both of you. Dr. Bennett was a good man but we must put the past away now, Marielle." He closed the scrapbook and set it aside. "To go back is only to open painful wounds. Let's go forward together." He put his arms around her. He remembered his own childhood. No loving mother or father. They were ripped from the world by the filthy Zionist pigs. *Thanks be to Allah,* he thought, *for the Madrassas where I learned to turn the tragedy of my childhood into productive anger! Into Jihad!*

He wished he could've known his boy but the fact that he died among the 9/11 martyrs gave him great comfort and a sense of pride.

Ghani fell asleep in her arms again. *How sweet he looks as he sleeps, and how tragic it is that his hatred has caused so much harm,* she thought.

She knew that if changes weren't made in the world to give all people a place at the global table, other Ghanis would rise up. She felt an emptiness and deep sadness about what she had to do. She imagined the moments when the device ignited. Would anyone even know what hit them? She tried to stop having such morbid thoughts, but they filled her head.

After a while, exhausted, she fell asleep. She dreamed of her new horse. She decided to call him Hope.

In the morning she was awakened by June. Ghani had been called back to Yemen. He was meeting with high-ranking Al Qaeda and Hezbollah members who were trying desperately to regroup. "How do you know?" Marielle asked June.

"Oh, Ali told me," she replied.

Marielle couldn't believe how careless these people were becoming and it worried her especially since Ali was vital to her mission and June was such a fanatic.

June was happy. Her brother, Ali al Ilani, would be coming to the hotel today to see her. He wanted to meet Marielle. He arrived in time for lunch, and the three of them went downstairs to the dining room to eat. Marielle was shocked to see Leron Yitzaki dressed in traditional Arab garb, sitting at a table across the room with several other men who looked like Arabs but who must have been Mossad. *What a den of vipers,* Marielle mused.

Ali looked at Leron long enough for Marielle to be made uncomfortable by it. *What a nest of intrigue I am in,* she thought. She looked at no one, even asking June, "How am I doing? I've kept my eyes down and looked at no man." Poor, simple June was so pleased that Marielle was actually practicing to be a good Muslim wife, she shut up for the rest of the lunch.

Ali wanted his sister to return to the States right away. He did not want her to participate in the movement. He loved her, and truly feared for her life. Marielle thought he was about to confide in her about himself so she knocked over a glass of juice, which spilled all over June.

"Oh June, I'm so sorry," she said. "I haven't had much sleep the last two nights, so I'm clumsy. Here, take our key and go up to the suite and change your dress." June left the table to change.

Marielle said, "For God's sake, Ali, you can't trust your sister. She has a romanticized view of Islam and lives only to destroy the Jews. She would betray you and me in a minute and compromise our mission. She's a problem. Tell her nothing except go home. I agree with you. She should not get involved in any of this. You are her brother; order her to go home." Then she asked Ali, "Do you know why Leron is in Dubai?"

"He is watching you," he said.

June returned to the table having changed her clothes. "What were you two talking about?" she asked suspiciously.

"I was telling Marielle that someone else would accompany her to Yemen. You are returning to New York," he said, flatly.

"But Ali . . . " she implored.

"Listen, Hana," he said, using her Lebanese name. "I am your brother and I do not want you involved here in my life. I do not trust you completely. You were raised by Americans. You must obey me and prove you truly understand Islam. You are a woman—do you understand? Only a woman. I have made a decision."

June was crushed but lowered her head in deference to male authority. Marielle and June went upstairs to pack. June was devastated. Marielle tried to assuage her anxiety. "If you obey him now, he'll give you another opportunity to serve," she told her. "Try to accept his will, June. Remember you told me the will of the man in the family is law. It is Allah's will that you obey."

"What do you know about Allah?" she snapped. "You—who even as we speak are corrupting and polluting our beloved leader with your willful ways." June had begun to hate Marielle and everything she stood for.

Marielle was secretly amused and tried not to laugh. June didn't like it any more than any woman would, but she accepted her brother's wishes. The next morning she said goodbye to Marielle, and was on her way back to the States. Marielle gave her two boxes of delicious dates, and some presents she purchased in the *souk* for Caroline.

Earlier she spoke briefly to Caroline to let her know she was well, and described Hope. Caroline said she was looking forward to seeing pictures of the new horse. She was being unusually supportive. "Mom, Hope sounds like quite a horse. You must be thrilled. I bet you can't wait to take a few fences with him. He must be really something for you to call him your dream horse, considering all the wonderful champions we've owned. Either Hope is the best piece of horseflesh on the planet or you've gone daffy. I really envy you. I'm getting as big as a house now and couldn't ride if my life depended on it."

"I love you," Marielle said, "and ditto for that baby of yours."

"Mine and Patrick's," she reminded her mother laughing. "Call me soonest, Mummy."

"I will," Marielle promised.

Marielle had to get ready to go to Yemen. Ali returned as she was packing and with him was the woman who would accompany her. "This is Nyela Jawad. She is a Palestinian and a brave member of Hamas and a veteran of many missions. It is her honor to serve you, Madame."

"Nice to meet you, Nyela," Marielle said. "We have a lot to do before we can leave. Ali, is my horse going along with us today?" Ali said he would look into it. Nyela began to help her pack. She was about five foot seven and very muscular and looked like she worked out with fifty-pound weights. Marielle smiled. She guessed Nyela was a sort of female bodyguard.

"Once we get close to the Yemeni border you will need your chador," she told Marielle softly.

"Will you wear one, too?" Marielle asked curiously.

"Yes. All women wear them in public. I know you are an honorary man, Madame, but until you are safe within the complex, we want you to be covered. We will be flying into Saudi Arabia to a small airstrip from where we will drive to the complex."

"Where exactly are we going?" Marielle asked her curiously.

"I don't know, Madame. Only those who need to know are aware of the exact whereabouts of it."

She felt slightly uneasy as she, Nyela, and six heavily armed men left for the airport. This time they didn't go through any checkpoints. Their Mercedes took them directly out to the little jet which was waiting for them at the far end of the tarmac. Marielle noticed a cargo plane nearby and saw Hope being unloaded from a trailer, fighting the men who tried to move him to the plane's ramp. As he balked they whipped him cruelly. Marielle was furious.

"Drive me over there immediately," she demanded. The driver looked to the six men. "I am an honorary man," she commanded. "Take me over there immediately or I will have Ghani Irabi deal harshly with all of you," she threatened.

"Obey her," one of the men said. "That is Madame's horse." In a second they were there and she jumped out of the Mercedes.

"Stop," she said angrily, taking the horse's lead in her hands, ripping it away from the man who beat him. The guard explained it was Madame's horse and he shouldn't have whipped it. The guard asked her if she wanted the man whipped for what he had done.

"No," she said. "Just tell him to get out of the way. I'll load my horse myself." Marielle knew horses and realized the roar of the planes' engines were spooking him. She asked them to shut down the engines. Then she blindfolded the horse with her Hermès scarf and calmed him down by leading him around a few times. As they approached the ramp, Hope easily went up into the plane. She made sure he felt comfortable inside, coaxing him to eat his oats. She then decided she'd rather fly in the cargo plane with him. She told the guard, "I'll meet you in Saudi Arabia. Please get my belongings from the other plane."

"Yes, Madame," he said. "One of us must accompany you so you can communicate. These people don't speak English or listen to women."

"Then you come along," said Marielle. "What is your name?"

"Mahmoud, Madame. Mahmoud el Said." He returned to the jet and told the others, "Madame wants to fly with her horse. Give me her chador and bags; I am going with her."

The private jet was the first to take off, then the cargo plane. It rattled like crazy as it slid down the landing strip, and then they were in the air. Hope was a little jittery, but settled down and started to eat. Mahmoud explained to the pilot that Marielle was a very important woman. Ghani Irabi had made her an honorary man. The pilot argued that she couldn't sit in the flight deck with Mahmoud and himself, even if she was an honorary man, as he never heard of such a thing. He said she could sit on the bales of hay next to her horse. Marielle was just as happy to stay near Hope anyway. Two stablemen were in the rear with the horse as well. The plane's interior was very open so they could see the private jet in front of them in the distance.

A few minutes passed and then there was a huge explosion. It was the private plane.

Marielle couldn't believe what she saw. The explosion caused their plane to shake as it lit up the sky like Fourth of July fireworks. Their pilot lost control momentarily as he veered their plane out of the path of falling debris.

She tried to calm Hope as soon as the plane stabilized. He fell down and had trouble getting up. His nostrils flared. She spoke softly to him, and after he regained his footing she saw his pastern was swelling. She asked Mahmoud if they had a cold pack in the first aid kit. She removed Hope's bandages. It appeared to be a sprain and nothing serious, she thought, as she felt his leg.

Mahmoud thanked Allah while he looked for the cold pack. As Marielle waited she thought of the people on the private jet; alive one minute and dead the next. She realized then and there that her life was unquestionably on the line. Red Connors had warned her that life had no meaning whatsoever to these zealots. She was truly frightened.

As soon as he found the cold pack, Mahmoud ran to the back and gave it to Marielle, who applied it to Hope's leg.

Mahmoud explained to her that there were many militants who were not happy that Ghani was going to take a Western wife, and an American at that. "You Madame, saved my life by asking me to stay with you. I owe my life to you now, and by Allah I will always protect you. I will even give up my manhood to be your protector," he said, respectfully.

She didn't understand what Mahmoud meant by giving up his manhood, but she thanked him for his sincerity. Marielle truly liked the people in the Middle East. They had so many admirable qualities. She was saddened by the hatred that drove the region down so destructive a path.

When they reached the Saudi landing strip, she put on her

chador. She waited inside the plane as Mahmoud went outside to see if it was safe for them to disembark. Ghani and more than seventy heavily armed men were waiting for them. Marielle herself unloaded Hope into the waiting horse trailer. The driver of the trailer was a Mujahadim fighter who was also a great horseman. He watched her handle the stallion and indeed understood how such a woman deserved to be an honorary man. He would care for her horse as though it were his own.

Once Hope was loaded Marielle went over to Ghani. She hugged him, an act usually reserved for a private place in his world. His behavior when it came to her worried some of his associates. This had led to the failed attempt on her life which had cost many good men in the explosion. Women didn't count here, so Nyela wasn't even considered a loss.

Ghani was relieved to see Marielle safe. He was amused by her love for the horse he gave her, but would not rest until whoever was responsible for the sabotage that almost killed her was put to a long and painful death. It took almost seven hours to drive to the complex. An exhausted Marielle fell asleep in his arms.

The complex was hidden between the Red Sea cities of Hudaydah and Sana. It was an oasis in the middle of the rugged desert.

Once inside the steel gates, they got on the elevator that took them down several hundred feet into the complex. The rooms of their quarters were beautiful and filled with priceless *objets d'art,* both Western and Islamic. The bedroom was enormous and overlooked an incredible indoor garden with grow lights that simulated the sunshine and outdoors. The ceilings were more than thirty feet high, painted blue like the sky. There was even an Olympic-size swimming pool.

Ghani explained to Marielle that her things were going to be delivered in a few days. His security people had to check them.

Marielle prayed Morty's plastic coating would work and confuse the radioactive material detectors.

"Someday, my love, when we have brought the Great Satan to his knees, and destroyed Israel, we will live anywhere you want in the world," he said lovingly.

"Yes, my darling, yes," she answered as she fell asleep that night.

The following morning he brought her breakfast as he had done at the hotel in Dubai.

"My angel, it is so wonderful to have you here. All these years we've been apart, no other woman has meant anything to me. I have lived only for justice for my people," he said sincerely.

Marielle understood and felt pity for the plight of the Palestinians too. But you can't get justice with murder and terror. If only there was a way to peacefully stop the killing and the hatred. But there wasn't. She knew what she had to do.

For the time being, though, she was able to put that out of her mind and decided that, for these last few weeks, she would live a lifetime. She'd bask in the glow of their star-crossed love until she did her sad duty. She realized she was not much different from the hijackers and murderers of 9/11, waiting to commit a violent act, waiting to break God's commandments in the name of God himself. It was all so ironic.

If it's for our side, it's for good and God. But no violence is right and in her heart she knew it. Would she be punished more harshly by God in the end because she really understood God meant "Thou Shall Not Kill." She wondered.

"Oh Ghani," Marielle said, "whatever happened to your admiration for Mahatma Gandhi and Dr. Martin Luther King?"

He looked at her ruefully. "Sweet Marielle, don't clutter your pretty head. You cannot understand the code we live by; the Code of Hamurabi."

Marielle knew the Code of Hamurabi: an eye for an eye and a

tooth for a tooth. *A father for a son,* she thought. Yes, perhaps she too wanted justice; justice for John Paul and all the others.

She thought of President Bush, a man she greatly admired. What other president in the world would have dropped food for the starving innocents of war on a land that harbored the murderers of your people? No, she resolved, no other people are as kind and compassionate as we Americans. So proud we stand up. We have reason to be proud. I abhor killing but it must be done to stop this madness.

Ghani was saying something. "I'm sorry, I didn't hear you," she said.

"Where were you, my love? You were lost in your thoughts."

"I was missing John Paul, our son."

"Try not to dwell on his death. He died with our martyrs."

Marielle couldn't help herself. She lashed out momentarily, releasing her true feelings. "Ghani, for God's sake, he wasn't a martyr. He knew nothing of Islam. He was a loving, innocent American boy working hard, realizing his dreams and doing good in the world. Murder can never be justified. Although I know you did not intentionally kill our son, violence is violence no matter who is wielding the sword or the gun, or the bomb. What has happened to you? What has become of your words that I have cherished all these years? You told me, 'The greatest love of God is to love your fellow man.' Don't you remember?"

He turned his back on her.

"That was a lifetime ago. If we are to move forward we will never speak of politics again," he said brusquely.

Chapter Fifteen

GHANI DECIDED TO SHOW MARIELLE THE ENTIRE complex. It was almost 900,000 square feet, and part of it contained a huge computer network that kept them in touch with their supporters; both financial and fighting forces worldwide. There were closed-circuit television and listening devices in every room, even in her bathroom, he told her. "Someone is constantly monitoring to make sure no moles are present here. The war room is as state of the art as the one in the Pentagon."

Marielle was stunned by the extent of their global information-gathering network. "We actually have a mole in the CIA," he added smugly. "She tells us of all joint intelligence efforts between the Israelis and the U.S."

This alarmed Marielle, but she continued to smile, undaunted. She would have to be ready for anything at any moment.

"We are jointly developing weapons of mass destruction with Iraq. The material for this project really comes from China, but they don't realize it because China is helping its ally, North Korea, and their nuclear program. The North Koreans sell information to Iraq. This way we will soon have a weapon of mass destruction," he proudly told her.

"Do you mean actual missiles with nuclear warheads?" she questioned.

"Yes, that's exactly what I mean. The coordination of all cells within this Jihad is done through one computer with a program that sends orders in code to our various leaders around the world who, in turn, coordinate the attacks. Monies are distributed from Bank Sarazin in Brazil worldwide through this same computer hookup. It's simple and effective. Everything is linked by computer." He laughed now. "The West is fixated on bin Laden, but he is just one of many."

"How many?" asked Marielle, hoping there was some way to get this information out before she blew the complex to kingdom come.

"You will meet my fellow freedom fighters in three weeks when they come to the festivities leading up to our wedding and the simultaneous attacks on New York, Boston, Los Angeles, Chicago, Washington, D.C., London, Berlin, Paris, and Moscow."

As he rattled off the cities that would be hit, he looked like a madman. His eyes were glazed over with more hatred than Marielle had ever seen in her life. She started to worry about Caroline. Ghani wanted Caroline and her husband to attend the wedding, but Patrick wouldn't allow her to travel so far in her condition. He was concerned that such a long trip could complicate her pregnancy. Marielle would have to think of something to protect Caroline just in case her mission wasn't successful. She couldn't stand the thought of both her children being killed by terrorist attacks, not to mention the coming grandchild.

They continued walking through the complex. Marielle wore a beige Armani pant suit with a long-sleeved pale green blouse underneath. She had on her favorite comfortable Gucci loafers. Her long, silky hair, freshly washed, but not set, framed her still-exquisite face.

Ghani led her into a large conference room filled with Middle

Eastern men, some with head coverings, and others dressed Western style. They all paid homage to him. He was clearly the commander in chief.

"This is Marielle Bennett. She is an honorary man. You will treat her as such or you will be removed from my complex."

She realized she had to rise to the occasion and be worthy of the part he wanted her to play. "Good morning, gentlemen. Ghani has bestowed great honor on me and I am grateful for his trust and love. I want to be useful to the poor and downtrodden people of the world who seek justice and a decent human life. Like my future husband, I will seek to give the Palestinian people a homeland. I want to feed the poor, tend the sick, and bury the dead. I want to educate children so that they can understand and serve the teachings of Allah. I feel my place here is with the women of the complex. That is how I will serve my husband-to-be. In the future I will respect your long-standing traditions." The interpreter translated her words for the men. "My darling Ghani, it is my right as an honorary man to decide this, is it not? Except for riding my precious horse, Hope, I will prefer to live as my husband's wife; nothing more."

He was never more proud of her. She excused herself and told him she would return straightaway to the private quarters. As she left every man rose.

She made her way through the intricate maze of long corridors when she was suddenly confronted by a sneering man whom she instantly recognized. Terror filled her, and for an instant she couldn't decide whether to turn and try to run back to Ghani or stand her ground and use her martial arts skills should it become necessary.

"We meet again, fair lady of the Maryland docks," he taunted her.

"Carlos," she said. "I thought you were in jail in Paris. I read about your capture in the newspaper. Did you escape?" She tried to make light conversation and read his body language to see if he meant her harm. She could not forget he once wanted to kill her.

Carlos, balding now with grey at the temples, roared with laughter. "I don't believe for a moment you are so innocent or naïve. You play them all," he said derisively, his eyes boring into her. "All except for me."

Marielle tried to control her nerves. She was gripped by a clutching fear and she felt her cheeks and lips begin to quiver.

"The man in the Paris jail is someone we created with plastic surgery to look like me; a decoy we've thrown like a bone to the barking dogs of Interpol," he said arrogantly.

"You have to excuse me," she said, moving forward. "I have a lot of unpacking to do. My things have just arrived and I'm in the middle of decorating our home," she explained matter-of-factly. She sighed as she quickly made her way down the hall. She was afraid to look back and didn't know if she was imagining his eyes still on her, or if she was just scared to death.

Ghani continued his meeting in the conference room. The most militant and religious zealot, the radical Pakistani cleric Sheik Jilani, spoke. "Ghani, many of us doubted your judgment when you brought this woman within our midst. But now we see that you have chosen wisely, and I congratulate you. You are a lucky man to have found a Western woman who knows her place."

Ghani was angered by the audacity of Jilani, the man whom he suspected of the attempt on Marielle's life in the attack which also cost him his plane and the lives of several trusted associates. "Her place is at my side," Ghani barked. In Ghani's mind, Jilani's fate was already sealed. Immediately after the meeting he ordered the sheik's death.

Sheik Jilani met with a terrible accident that afternoon when a faulty electric wire in his quarters burned him beyond recognition. The fire itself was contained in his faction's section of the complex.

Killed with the sheik were his four wives, seven children, and three bodyguards.

While Ghani was pleased by the news, he nevertheless feigned sadness to the top officials in his pseudo cabinet, and returned to his private quarters to be with Marielle. He expected her to be horrified over the loss of life when he told her what he had just done. She told him, however, she respected his actions and understood that some people must die for the greater good.

She quickly changed the subject. "I didn't realize Carlos was here," she said. "It gave me quite a start when I ran into him. I wish you had told me he was here."

"Darling, he must have just arrived," Ghani said.

She had been arranging her furniture. The large grandfather clock was already in place by the entrance to Ghani's personal study. "I see you brought the old clock from Oyster Bay Cove. It brings back many fond memories. I am happy to have you surrounded by familiar things," he said, smiling.

Marielle put the compact with her makeup articles in her handbag. No one would suspect this compact was the trigger for a bomb. *How easy this will be,* she mused. *Everything is now in place.* She hugged her bear.

For a brief moment she thought about setting the bomb off right then and there. It was Ghani who she had come to kill, after all. But the knowledge that so many operatives were coming to the festivities, providing the opportunity to destroy *so* many of the movement's leaders in one fell swoop, made her decide to wait. She felt strangely excited by the power she held; the power to punish those who took the life of her son. Though she knew she could be discovered at any moment, she didn't worry about the mission being completed. She decided that she would carry the compact with her so she could detonate it at will. It all seemed so surreal.

She felt relieved to know that she would live a little longer. The few extra days might give her the time to learn some answers should there be any. She wanted to understand Ghani and what had gone so wrong with him. Had she been truthful, she would have admitted to herself she also wanted to love a little longer. Suddenly she thought, a lifetime crammed into moments. She shuddered.

"Are you all right?" he inquired.

"I'm just cold, sweetheart," she said, trying to cover her fear.

"I will adjust the air. You know I like it cool, but I want you to be comfortable," he said, concerned.

"That's okay. I think I'll go riding. That will get my juices flowing." She laughed half-heartedly.

"That's a good idea," he said. "This has been a big adjustment for you. It will clear your mind." He kissed her neck tenderly as she began to get dressed.

She rode nearly every day. Most days she dressed early because by 9:00 AM it had become too hot to ride. At 4:00 AM her alarm would go off and she'd go up and away in the elevator that took her to the surface. Mahmoud would meet and drive her. She never knew that the limp he developed right after they arrived in Yemen was due to his recent castration. In order to be trusted alone with the wife, or wife-to-be, of a leader, one must not be a whole man. Mahmoud made his sacrifice willingly, for in his own way, he loved the beautiful woman who had saved his life.

Mahmoud drove her the ten minutes to the stable where the Mujahadim fighters kept their horses. All the stalls had fans for the animals' comfort. Hope got extra special treatment. These hardened Afghan fighters never saw a woman who could ride like Marielle. She was a more skillful horsewoman than most of them, and they admired her. In a short period of time she had become something of a legend to the men. Some thought she was bewitching Ghani Irabi, but after Sheik Jilani's death, no one dared even whisper their opposition to her.

Marielle loved to race with the Mujahadim riders in spite of Mahmoud's deep concern that she could be hurt. "Madame, these men ride like the devil across the sand," he warned. "The horses will kick it up and blind you."

"Not if I'm in front," she chided him and in front she'd go, Hope's hoofs thundering across the desert leaving the others in a cloud of dust as he stretched out and galloped like the wind.

One day, Adan, the leader of the group, caught up with her. She slowed up so he could ride alongside.

"Follow me," he said. "I will take you to our secret place."

He turned his mount and went up the side of a steep rocky hill, which went almost straight up and was a difficult climb, even for Hope. When they reached the top they descended to a hidden canyon with strange ancient rock formations dotting what appeared to be an old, well-worn trail. Marielle noticed the absence of life in the desert wasteland except for the hawks which continually circled above them.

After they rode several miles, they came to an oasis. To Marielle's surprise, there was an old well there with water pure enough to drink. It stood in the shadow of the crumbling ruins of what appeared to have been a fortress. Its huge wooden doors were still intact.

Marielle assumed the water came from an underground spring. She wondered how anyone figured out there was water below. The men drew water from the well and shared their cup with Marielle and Mahmoud. They offered her bread with a spread that tasted like hummus. After they ate they rested.

Marielle taught Hope to follow her like a faithful dog. She unsaddled him and they began to play together, the horse running circles around her. When they were tired they rested in the shade of some straggly trees. Hope loved it when she kissed him on the soft part of his muzzle and scratched his huge chest.

Mahmoud tried to copy his mistress, but his horse Ayazen ran off into the sand dunes. It took the better part of the morning for Adan and his men to catch her. They were annoyed and told Mahmoud he was a "stupid goat" for letting the mare get away and ruin their rest. Marielle chuckled, but Mahmoud was utterly humiliated. *These men take themselves so seriously,* she thought, amused.

Just before the end of the first week, Ali al Ilani showed up in Yemen with a woman companion for Marielle. It seemed Ghani met with Ali in Dubai on other business and Ali asked if Marielle might be lonely for female company. Ghani, who thought of nothing but making her happy, fell for this Israeli ruse to get one of their agents into the complex. When Ali brought her, he was invited to stay on a few days to help with the preparations for the party preceding the wedding, as well as the details for the global assault Ghani planned.

Golda Guetta, Marielle's new female companion, was a major in Israeli Intelligence and had been briefed in Washington by the CIA. She was there to get vital files out of the complex before it was destroyed. Her Arabian identity said she was Rima Saad, a senior member of Hamas. This was partially true as she had been undercover for the past seven years.

Ghani told Marielle he arranged for Rima to come because other than his companionship, she had only her horse and Mahmoud. He didn't want her to be lonely.

She wasn't sure if she could really trust Rima or if she had been planted by Ghani or Ghani's enemies to spy on her. She continued to spend as much time as she could riding the rugged terrain with the Mujahadim fighters. She knew preparations were at a full court press for the parties leading up to the wedding, which was to take place Sunday, December 30, 2001.

Ghani had a small evergreen tree flown in and planted in the indoor garden. It was a Colorado blue spruce about five feet tall. He also had decorations for it if Marielle chose to have a Christmas tree in her private quarters. He knew how much she adored Christmas, but Marielle decided against the decorations. She didn't really feel in the mood for Christmas.

On December 23, she returned from riding early and came upon Rima in Ghani's private study. She was downloading information from his computer. She said, "Marielle, you know I'm on your side. I'm working with Leron. You weren't supposed to see this."

"How can you be so careless?" Marielle said, panic stricken. "Jesus, you've already been detected! They'll be here any moment. Get out of here. I'll say I was trying to e-mail my daughter Caroline. Anyone who touches that thing sets off an alarm in the computer room. I'll say I forgot to enter the code. Oops, sorry—now get going," she ordered.

Rima left the room and as she headed down the hall she was grabbed by two Pakistani guards. Ghani, who was on his way to his quarters, told the guards to bring Rima in. She had disabled the room's cameras so they had no visual or audio, and had reinstated them before she departed, leaving Marielle to get her out of trouble.

"Oh Ghani," Marielle laughed. "I forgot to put in the stupid code you gave me before I e-mailed Caroline. Is there a problem?"

Ghani's chief security officer said, "We have no video or audio, sir, on what happened. Someone must have tampered with the equipment. The feed was temporarily suspended so we have nothing. We saw nothing." Ghani was angry.

"You don't need to see anything in this room," he said harshly. He pulled the camera violently from the wall. "Tomorrow I will put all of my sensitive files in the war room. My bride needs her privacy and doesn't need your paranoia. I am going to Dubai. Leave her and her companion alone. She can e-mail her daughter and it's not your business," he growled. He had seven guards stand watch outside their quarters to see to her safety, including Mahmoud who would remain inside with Marielle.

"Guard her with your lives or all of your families will pay for it

171

with theirs," he threatened. Turning to Marielle he said, "Darling, I am sorry to ask you to stay in for the next few days, at least until after Christmas. We are engaged in some very serious business now. I don't want to have to worry about you, my precious one. I'll be back tomorrow in the early afternoon. We have many guests arriving then, so be rested for the formal dinner tomorrow night. I promise after our wedding you can ride Hope all you want."

Marielle sadly accepted the fact that she would never see Hope again. *How near the day of our destiny,* she thought. The guards were all on edge, and even Mahmoud seemed anxious.

"Madame, something is afoot and it's not good," he said. "There is much dissension in the inner circle. People are on edge about Sunday, your wedding day of joy. Many of the martyrs will go to their deaths in the planned attacks. Syria alone will suffer the most casualties. An Iraqi fighter plane carrying a nuclear bomb intended for Tel Aviv will be disguised as a Syrian domestic flight to Jordan. My brother is going to be the pilot on that plane."

Rima and Marielle exchanged knowing glances. Marielle knew that Rima had to get this information to her superiors, but there was no way for her to leave the complex. She also had to finish downloading Ghani's files before they could be destroyed. Marielle decided to invite her to enjoy a swim in the indoor pool. The sound of the running water would prevent anyone from overhearing them, and the blue spruce blocked the camera. She told Rima they could send a coded message in an e-mail to Caroline. The CIA was monitoring Caroline's e-mail messages in case something went wrong. Marielle would use two key words in case something happened, and Leron was, no doubt, getting copies of all these e-mails as well.

Marielle said, "We'll send whatever you are taking out through an attachment to the e-mail. Come on, Rima. There's little time left. Ghani will return and move all the files you're after. We can't waste a minute."

They downloaded the files. It took all of a few minutes. Then Marielle sent the e-mail to Caroline.

"Please set the device and come with me. Ali will be here soon with a story about my mother being critically ill. Get out with us," Rima pleaded.

"How can I? Ghani might become suspicious and the device must be armed. There are only thirty minutes after the device is armed before it explodes. This is my destiny. I have accepted it for the good of the world."

"Thank you for saving Israel," Rima said.

"I'm not only saving Israel; I am saving Palestine too. There must be a decent life for all people of the world; not just the people who are like us, but everyone. If you truly want to do something for me," Marielle said, "begin to love your fellow man as you love yourself. The greatest love of God is to love your fellow man."

Marielle believed those words, the words of her lover. It seemed so long ago. But Rima was herself the product of the fanatical hatred she learned as a child. Such hatred dies hard. She, like most Israelis, wanted Israel for Jews, and the Palestinians were her sworn and hated enemy. She would have no trouble killing every last one of them and, in fact, had killed several as part of her undercover work.

She did not understand Marielle at all. Marielle was there to destroy Islam on the one hand, but wanted the Palestinians to have a homeland on the other. *It's them or us,* Rima thought, *and nothing is going to change my mind.*

But Marielle's words, "The greatest love of God is to love your fellow man," kept repeating in her ears.

Damn you, Marielle. What are you doing to me? I don't give a shit about the Palestinians, Rima thought. But she knew in her heart that Marielle was speaking the words of God. And more important, the will of God. Rima was ashamed, and realized Marielle was right.

As Rima left, she realized this woman lived her Christianity and set an example that was an honor to follow. *How tragic it is that she will die. If only I could save her somehow, some way.* Now she understood why even Leron held Marielle in such high regard. Even if you didn't agree with her. You had to respect her courage.

Rima still had a lot to do before she could leave the complex. She would see Marielle again before she and Ali left, and vowed to try to convince Marielle again to set the device and leave with them.

Meanwhile in the war room Ghani was at work. "Ghani, my friend," Carlos said as they embraced, "I have come to share in the glory to come. I cannot believe you have brought the American here. What were you thinking? You should have let me kill her. It was a mistake to let her live."

Ghani was shocked to hear his friend speak of his Marielle that way. "I won't hear this. Stop right now," he demanded.

"She will be our undoing," Carlos went on. "She escaped me again when she decided to ride in the cargo plane with the horse." Ghani was incredulous and outraged as he realized it was Carlos and Sheik Jilani who had conspired against him, not just Jilani alone. "She is not here out of love for you. A woman like that doesn't move to Yemen and give up her life for love. She has an agenda. I am certain of it, I can smell it. Ask yourself this: Why were the surveillance cameras down? This is a plot. It reeks of the CIA. We killed her son; she wants our lives in return."

"It was my son who died. Mine and Marielle's," Ghani said. "Carlos, we have been closer than brothers for forty years, but she is my happiness. She is more important to me than anyone. Why can't you just accept her as I do? She came here to grieve, to let me know I had a son; our son, John Paul, who died with the martyrs. I contacted her."

Carlos grabbed Ghani by the shoulders. "You are a lovesick fool. You'd let a woman come between us—our cause," he said.

Ghani was at a boiling point. He pulled free. "You, Carlos, are an empty man, incapable of love."

Carlos lunged toward Ghani's throat. "I'll kill you before you ruin everything," he growled. The two men struggled for what seemed like forever. Carlos was the much more experienced fighter and he quickly gained an advantage over Ghani. But Ghani was fueled by pure rage. First Carlos had tried to kill his beloved Marielle and now he dared to come after him. Ghani fought with a determination that could not be overcome.

In the end Ghani and his rage proved to be too much for Carlos. After breaking his neck, Ghani gently lowered Carlos's lifeless body to the floor, asking himself, *What have I done? I have killed my best friend,* he sobbed. Tears streamed down his face.

He felt confused. *Could Carlos have been right?* he asked himself. "She poisons me," he cried. His love for Marielle, however, was so strong he listened to his heart and not his reason. "No, Carlos no," he told the dead man. "She is my angel, my life. You were wrong. Nothing will come between us. She is my destiny."

Chapter Sixteen

ON MONDAY, THE 24TH OF DECEMBER, GHANI RETURNED late in the afternoon with several guests. He spent about an hour getting them settled in. Marielle decided, since it was Christmas Eve, to plan a quiet dinner for the two of them and then they'd watch some old movies. She loved *Miracle on 34th Street,* the old one with Maureen O'Hara and Natalie Wood as the sweet little girl. Ghani adored the opera *Turandot,* and Marielle had an old tape with Pavarotti in the lead. They both enjoyed hearing him sing "Nessum Dorma"; it was their favorite aria.

Ghani's chef, Omar, was from Egypt. He worked for a large hotel chain and traveled all over the world. In his early career, he was sous chef at the Beverly Hills Hotel, and he was a nephew of a famous Egyptian actor's. Marielle loved his tasty fare and asked him to make a special Christmas Eve dinner for them to enjoy alone. He arranged for turkey with stuffing, her favorite asparagus magritte, Canadian sweet potatoes, and, for dessert, flaming baked Alaska. She had a case of Ghani's favorite Cristal Champagne shipped in with her belongings.

Omar was a jolly fellow who didn't take much of what went on too seriously. He called the mullahs "bags of wind" behind their backs, and kept a supply of bacon for Marielle's breakfasts and her BLT sandwiches. He was going to visit his wife who lived in Paris for New Year's. "Right after I make your wedding the most spectacular food fest ever," he laughed. "Mind you, your wedding cake will have eight tiers. It will be fit for a queen, I promise you."

Marielle hugged him. "Thank you," she gushed. "I am looking forward to my wedding day." She tried not to think of the innocent people like Omar who would die that day. If she did she would go crazy. So she put it out of her mind and tried to live as happily as would a woman who was finally going to marry the love of her life.

It was 6:30 PM when Ghani came to the private quarters. He was tired and stressed, but the sight of her was all he needed to feel better. He knew right away by the twinkle in her eyes that she was up to something. She giggled.

"Ah, my love," he said, "what have you planned for us?"

"It's a surprise, dearest," she said coyly, "but I thought you might join me for a bath. I'll give your back a massage just as you like it." A back massage always led him to make love. "Then I've got a present for you." She took out a small, blue Tiffany box.

"I've got something for you, too," he smiled. "When do you want to open them?"

"At midnight, when Christmas Day dawns," she replied romantically.

They got into their large bathing pool and embraced in the warm water. They were so in love with each other still, after all the years. She had left the knowledge of whom and what he had become in some distant place, and for the moment she allowed herself to live and love, for she knew there would be only a few more tomorrows.

When they got out of the bath he stretched on the bed face down. She tickled his ribs and began slowly, gently scratching his back with her long, beautiful nails. Then she took some massage oil and kneaded his shoulders and neck. Ghani was so tense around his neck muscles. "Relax my love," she cooed. "Clear your mind and let me make you feel good."

He needed her like some people need drugs. He rolled over and took her in his arms, kissing her face and neck, exciting her once again. By the time they finished, it was ten minutes to eight. "Oh Ghani," she said, "Omar will be here with his staff to serve our dinner. We had better hurry and dress."

"Don't be silly; we're at home. Put on one of your fancy dressing gowns," he ordered. "I'll wear my cashmere robe. After we eat, woman, I want you back in that bed."

They laughed. In these moments all was right with their world. The dinner was exquisitely presented by Omar. Ghani enjoyed the Cristal. Suddenly he jumped up and said, "Marielle, I can't wait till midnight. I want you to open your present."

"Oh all right; I'll open it now if you want me to," she said, resigned.

"Yes darling, I really want you to," he said as he handed her the beautifully wrapped package. The velvet box was exquisite. It had its own gold clasp. As she opened it she could hardly believe her eyes. He had given her a necklace to match her engagement ring. There must have been fifty carats of Canary diamonds surrounded by slightly smaller blue white diamonds, with a pair of earrings to match. She never saw anything more beautiful or extravagant in her life.

"Put them on, put them on."

"I need a little help, sweetheart." And as he closed the clasp he kissed her back. He loved her more than he ever loved anyone in his life. *Allah help me,* he thought. *I love her more than Islam.* They never got to watch *Miracle on 34th Street* or *Turandot,* and they fell asleep in each other's arms before Ghani got to open his present.

In the morning they had breakfast together as usual.

"Merry Christmas," he said as he gently woke her. While they ate he explained he'd be very busy meeting with some of the guests who arrived the day before.

"But you promised we'd have today together. You haven't even opened your present," she said pouting.

"Sorry, but I don't have time to play with you now," he said, almost a little annoyed with her. "Watch your movies, dear, and e-mail your daughter. How lucky you are that she and her husband are spending the holidays at their ski lodge in Sun Valley. Now we can both be relieved. It's too bad that they couldn't be here for our wedding, but they'll be okay." He kissed her forehead gently.

Marielle could not understand the coldness of this man who spoke about the unspeakable as if it were nothing.

He left her and she finished her breakfast alone. It was Christmas and she couldn't go to church, not that she'd feel right about going under the circumstances anyway. She couldn't ride Hope because Ghani thought some plot might be afoot, and she couldn't even go out of the private quarters because they were surrounded by mullahs who frowned on that sort of thing. In addition there were the "wacky packys" and trigger-happy maniacs from the Philippines, not to mention some high-ranking government people from Indonesia; all in all, the crème de la crème of international terror come home to roost.

Ghani was very disappointed that Saddam refused to come. He wouldn't attend anything to do with an American. Marielle assured Ghani that it probably had more to do with the fact that some Iranians and Saudis were coming than anything else.

Ghani also wished Osama would honor them but since 9/11 bin Laden's whereabouts were only known to himself. "Osama is a maverick and is lying low," Ghani confided. "He is really a bit of a coward who never marches into battle himself. He just makes the bullets, he didn't fire them."

If it weren't so unbelievable it would be laughable, considering a woman, an entity, which hardly exists in their eyes, was going to turn them all into toast in four days. *What power I have,* she thought. *Shall I blow them to kingdom come on Saturday evening after Ali and Rima leave, or shall I wait for Sunday morning?* she asked herself playing a sick mental game.

Marielle had already armed the bomb. Once she pressed the device, it would be over thirty minutes later. It had a fail-safe device so that if anyone tried to disarm it once it was set to go, it would detonate immediately. She was glad about that because you never knew when something could go wrong. She planned to tell Ghani what she did after it was too late to turn back. She wanted him to realize that what he did to his fellow man was evil, and if she had known what he was going to do with his life, the life she once saved, she would have led the Israelis straight to him.

Their son would be alive today had it not been for his attacks on the World Trade Center and her beloved country. She tortured herself for the answers to what turned the man she thought she knew so well into a monster whose hatred of Jews had cost so many innocent lives.

That kind of hatred sickened her. The hatred on both sides; the Israelis as well as the Palestinians fueled an out-of-control firestorm that was literally threatening the peace and security of the world. *How,* she wondered, *can Jews and Muslims and Christians manage to live peacefully in the United States, but be hell bent on killing each other in Israel and Palestine? Or for that matter the English and the Irish, or the Serbs and the Croats?*

In America, no one cares. People just get along. But in their own countries all hell breaks loose.

There must be a leader somewhere in this world who can stop

the violence and create peace. *It is all so unnecessary,* she thought. *All the pain and all the loss—for what?*

Marielle spent the rest of Christmas day reflecting on her own life and family. She prayed a lot, wishing Ghani would return and make the world go away once again. But that was not to be.

Chapter Seventeen

GHANI DID NOT RETURN TO THE PRIVATE QUARTERS
until 1:45 AM. Marielle was sleeping soundly, and he was careful not
to wake her. He had received some very disturbing news regarding
Ali al Ilani, and was trying to put it into perspective and figure out if
it had anything to do with Rima and what happened in his study.
He trusted Marielle completely, but tomorrow the woman who had
been their mole in the CIA was going to meet with one of their most
trusted operatives in Washington, D.C., bearing information about a
CIA plot against him. He was on edge and couldn't get to sleep. His
tossing and turning awakened Marielle. "What's wrong, dear?" she
asked groggily.

He told her that he fought bitterly with Carlos and that it had
resulted in Carlos's death.

"I am so upset that he forced me to choose between my love for
you and him. Even more important, my trusted love, my people
have photographs of Ali al Ilani meeting in Tel Aviv with two Israeli operatives and a representative of the CIA. As if that is not
enough, tomorrow our woman at the CIA will bring information
about a plot against me."

Marielle couldn't allow herself to be afraid. She knew something like this could happen. "My Lord," she said worriedly, "how awful. What can I do to help? What kind of plot? No one can harm you here. This place is a fortress. Do you think one of our guests could be an Israeli assassin? Oh darling, no wonder you don't want me to go out riding. They might try to kidnap me."

"Well," he said, "once we know what Irene Baroody has discovered, we'll be able to take the necessary steps."

"My God! That name sounds familiar. I think I know her. Didn't she work at the UN years ago as a translator?" she asked.

"Yes she did, before she got her security clearance and went to work for the CIA. Whatever information she has must be very sensitive and important. She's asking a million dollars for it. We pay her handsomely for every piece of information she gives us. She's in it for the money, not the cause; a disgusting woman. If she weren't so useful I would have had her terminated years ago."

Thank God, Marielle thought. *The bitch is waiting for her money before she spills the beans.*

Marielle knew she had to get a message to CIA headquarters. Red Connors told her to ask "if the cat was all right" if there was trouble. She decided to take a dangerous chance. *Reckless,* she thought, *but if I don't stop Irene Baroody, it will be necessary to detonate the bomb before all the targets arrive.* She laughed at herself. *I'm even beginning to use their stupid jargon.*

Ghani fell asleep and snored loudly. She got up and went into the study. She always kept her computer on so Caroline's e-mails would come right through. She began as she always did.

Dear Child and the Child Inside You,

I can't sleep. Ghani is worried that people are trying to kill us. An old acquaintance of mine whom you might have met years ago, Irene Baroody, who works at the CIA, has grave information for us. Hopefully she will

*tell us what's going on at the CIA. By the way, Caro-
line, is the cat all right? I miss you and love you. Sunday I will be Mrs. Ghani Irabi. I'll e-mail again in the
morning. Good night.*

Love,
Mummy

It was sent and received. *Well,* Marielle thought, *I'd better get to
sleep myself and tomorrow I will think of how to explain my e-mail, if
I have to.*

As she tried to go back to sleep, she looked at the compact which
she placed on the nightstand just in case, wondering if she should set
it off. *What if that Baroody bitch blows my cover?* She tried to calm
herself. *I'm in the cat bird seat. I must be patient and let all the rats into
the trap.*

That morning, Ghani left before breakfast arrived. Marielle was
terribly nervous, but put up a good front. She planned what she
would wear in the evening that day and the next, as she'd be dining
in the public area with Ghani and his guests.

For whatever reason no one paid any attention to the fact that
she e-mailed Caroline at 3:00 AM, or if they had, they said nothing
about it. She dressed for dinner in a long-sleeved Yves St. Laurent
full-length gown. She wore the diamond necklace and its matching earrings. Her hair was in a French twist with a large diamond
comb positioned on the side of it. The comb belonged to her
mother and Marielle hadn't worn her hair up like this for more
than twenty years.

Ghani rushed in to put on his Arabian tuxedo. He looked like
the prince of Araby, she thought. He was very distracted as Marielle
asked about what he learned that day. "Should we be frightened?"
she asked. "Should we postpone our wedding?"

"No, darling," he said. "You are the one thing I can believe in. Everything else is uncertain right now. I don't know whom I can trust. I am in a sea of lies and deception. You, Marielle, are the only true friend I have. You are the only one I can trust. My closest advisors are casting aspersions and clouds of doubt about you."

She was alarmed and it showed. She quickly covered. "I am very hurt to hear this, for no one has ever loved you more than I do."

"I know, Marielle. You risked your life for me. I will kill them all," he ranted, "all who oppose my life with you."

You are not so wrong, she thought. *They will all die soon.* She held his hand as they left for the dinner.

There were close to 100 people at dinner that evening, and Ghani told her that by Saturday night there would be 700 to 800 people, all there for the wedding and to witness Palestine ke Azadi ke Saka or, in English, "Operation Palestinian Homeland."

Marielle was the only woman seated at the main table in the dining room. The other wives were in a separate room. Ghani insisted that she sit at his side. He was on shaky ground and she could feel it. She kept her eyes only on him; at all other times she lowered them out of respect for the fanatical mullahs whom she felt might become so enraged as to shoot them both on the spot. Ghani was like most madmen before him; oblivious to those closest to him who might be planning some sort of coup.

After they dined, she asked if she might be excused to join the wives. Mullah Jazeera, one of the most rabid Pakistani clerics, said he would escort her to the other room. Ghani looked uneasy but Marielle put out her hand to the mullah. "Thank you," she said. "I am trying so hard to learn the ways and traditions of my husband so we can better serve Islam." Even the hardened hate-filled mullah was bowled over by the sincerity of Marielle's obvious feminine charms.

When they entered the room where the wives dined, he took

her over to his own wife who just arrived from Paris. "Woman," he said, addressing her in a very demeaning tone of voice, "welcome Marielle to your group of women. You may speak to her in English, and I want you to treat her as one of you." He smiled at Marielle, who couldn't believe it.

"Thank you Mullah Jazeera," she said, lowering her eyes like a good Muslim.

The mullah's wife was probably in her late sixties. Her hands were large and very bony, as though she had arthritis or something that enlarged her knuckles. You couldn't see much of her as she wore a chador, as did most of the wives. Marielle was surprised no one wore the burka. She asked why. One of the women laughed. "We are inside with other women. No need."

Marielle was sorry for them. Many had large families at home. *What will become of their children?* she thought. Marielle felt sad, and it was difficult to continue the charade. Among themselves, the women behaved like teenagers. They did not seem unhappy. *I guess you can get used to anything, and if this is all you've seen all your life, it must feel normal and natural.*

The mullah's wife said, "We are sorry your son was killed in the attack. But it is sad when the son of any mother is killed, is it not?" Marielle agreed, of course it was. "Then tell me why you Americans only cry for your sons? What about the Palestinian sons who die every day at the hands of Israel, or the Lebanese sons, or the Iraqi sons? What about our sons? Are they less important than American sons?"

Marielle was without an answer, for it was true. No one cried for those fallen children; not like the cries heard around the world for those lost in 9/11. She realized this was not a black-and-white situation. *There is so much evil in the world,* she thought, *sometimes it's hard to know who is right and who is wrong.*

Again she thought of her president, and how the food gifts

meant survival to the Afghan people, and the help he gave the country once the Al Qaeda and the Taliban cancer was removed. "I try to pray for all the lost sons, and ask God for peace on earth," Marielle finally replied.

Mahmoud came into the room. "Madame," he said, "your master requests that you return now." She excused herself and left with him. As they walked back to the private quarters, Mahmoud told her to lock their bedroom door that night, and he gave her a small German Lugar. "Use this to defend yourself, Madame, if necessary. There are those who may make an attempt on your life."

"But Ghani will protect me."

"Ghani Irabi is no longer safe in his own bed."

When Ghani returned, Marielle told him what Mahmoud said and showed him the gun. He was not surprised, but told her not to fear. His most loyal guards were protecting them, and by morning those involved in any attempted insurrection would be dead.

Marielle did not sleep well at all, but her uneasiness had less to do with Ghani's internal revolt than her worry about Irene Baroody and what Ali al Ilani might say if they tortured him.

The next morning, Ghani went off to meetings and Marielle sent for Rima. As they often did, they exercised and swam. *My God,* she thought, *it's already the 27th.*

Marielle did not have good news for Rima as they sat under the pool's ornamental waterfall. She told Rima that Ali had been photographed with a known Mossad and CIA operative. "Once he arrives day after tomorrow, he will be tortured. Ghani told me they'll get what they can out of him. There's also a mole at the CIA. I sent a warning. I only hope they get her before it's too late."

"I can't believe you are so calmly blowing my life up," Rima said trying hard to laugh off the dire situation.

Marielle laughed too. "Rima, if you don't get out of here that's just what I'm going to do." She took her hand. "I'm trying to keep my sense of humor as long as I can. If you can get out before Ali comes, do it. I'm going to try to wait until all the guests are in the complex, but I'm going to have to act before they can get their hands on Ali."

Rima had never met anyone like this woman, a woman who gave up everything to come over to this God-forsaken hole in the desert to give her life to save people she didn't know and to protect cities in other countries. Rima was not as brave as Marielle, and she wanted to get out so she could head Ali off. He knew too much about Israeli intelligence and other deep-cover agents. One way or another, she had to stop them from learning anything from Ali.

The day flew by. Marielle was once again ready to join Ghani for dinner in the public area. It was now less than forty-eight hours until it would all be over. She walked around in a daze, going through the social motions, trying to seem relaxed and happy as a bride-to-be should be.

Ghani was very distant. "What is going on?" she asked him. "You leave me alone all day and you don't keep me informed of the developments you spoke about stateside."

"Darling, there is nothing to report. Our operative went to meet Irene Baroody with the money she demanded, but she didn't show up. We went to her house but she's gone, disappeared off the face of the earth," he said, puzzled. "We don't know what to make of it."

Marielle said she was sure they'd find her. His people knew what they were doing. She knew Red surely intercepted her e-mail to Caroline. *Thank God, and God bless America,* she thought.

The dinner was excellent. Omar was a genius when it came to putting on parties. Unfortunately no music was allowed in deference to the mullahs. The atmosphere was chilling. The men ate in silence and afterward talked in various languages. Marielle couldn't understand what they were saying, although from time to time she'd recognize Urdu. Whatever they were talking about, she knew it wasn't good.

Ghani returned with her to their quarters. He felt the underlying seeds of doubt growing in his mind. At once he hated himself for it. More than that he blamed the mullahs, for they were the ones who had started all this. But it was Carlos's death at his own hands that gnawed at him.

"Marielle, no matter what happens, I will always love you."

Then, looking straight into her eyes, he abruptly said, "Tell me now, is there anything I should know? I will protect you no matter what it is. I promise."

Would she be his undoing as Carlos predicted? He held her now, thinking he could so easily break her neck if, indeed, she were betraying him.

"Ghani, Ghani," she repeated as he realized she was trying to answer him. He'd been lost in the turmoil of his own fears and suspicions.

"Ghani, you know I always want to tell you I love you," she said, smiling.

"Please, please forgive me," he pleaded, breaking down. "I'm miles from here; I'm not myself. It will be all right; you will see. We'll be married and beyond this difficult time."

"Is it me? Are you having second thoughts about us?" Marielle asked, worried.

"Never," he reassured her. "I've waited what seems like an eternity to have you here by my side. Of course I want to marry you and share my life with you."

She felt relieved, as he swept her up into his strong arms and carried her off to bed.

Chapter Eighteen

THE FOLLOWING MORNING, MARIELLE WONDERED IF a relationship could be based solely on the physical. If so, they had a perfect one.

As Ghani brushed his teeth, he came out of the bathroom. He was very excited about Operation Palestinian Homeland. "My people surely will be free of Israel and be able to have a homeland in this New Year. The year 2002 will be the dawning of a new world for my people. And Marielle, you and I are at the heart of this. It will all begin here tomorrow when the martyrs collect the Russian suitcase bombs and leave for their target destinations. They will all be blessed and then they will depart. Will you honor me and stand by my side as the mullahs give them Allah's blessing in the holy ceremony?"

"Yes," she replied. "Of course we should be together for the holy ceremony."

He continued dressing. "As the martyrs fly toward their destinations all over the world this Sunday, we will exchange our vows and begin our first full day as man and wife *on* Monday, the eve of the New Year. The Palestinians' cries for freedom and a homeland will be clearly heard around the world as our bombs burst in the air and the infidels' cities are destroyed."

His eyes were wild with emotion now. *He's gone completely mad,* she thought. *Please God,* she said to herself, *give me strength for what must be done.* She looked at Ghani, realizing she loved this man, but at the same time realizing that he had to be stopped. She thought even the devil himself would feel disgusted at what he planned.

Marielle thought of Hope. She knew he would probably be safe since the radiation from the explosion would be contained underground. The complex had been built strong enough to withstand a nuclear explosion. That same strength would keep the force of the bomb from escaping the complex. She felt sad for Rima who'd probably never get out, and Ali would just be arriving when the bomb went off. She knew it took about fifteen minutes to walk from the private quarters to the great conference hall where the ceremony would be held. She would meet Ghani there. He already told her Mahmoud would bring her, as he would be too involved in the proceedings to come back to get her himself.

That would give her just enough time to stand face to face and confront the animal that the love of her life had seemed to become. She imagined telling him how it was all over. No more misguided martyrs and no more mothers weeping over lost sons. She tried to imagine the look on his face once he realized that his greatest plan would go unfulfilled. She wondered if he would die still loving her or if he would go to his grave hating her.

She bent down now to feel the panel in the clock where the device was housed. Her heart pounded. Three simple clicks, one long push, and there was no going back. Could she actually do this when the time came tomorrow to move past the point of no return? Or would her love of Ghani prevent her from carrying out her mission? She prayed for strength.

She thought of the man who said, "Let's roll" on one of the doomed 9/11 planes. He, too, knew there would be no going back. *When the time comes, we Americans do what we have to do. We're not martyrs; we're brave human beings who rise to any occasion when we have to. And that's why we'll win this war on terror in the end. Because right is might and we are the ones with the power and resolve to make the world a peaceful place for all.* But, the man on the plane was not about to kill the person he loved more than anyone else in the world. And while Marielle knew what had to be done, her heart was full of pain. Could she do it? Or would her feelings for this man paralyze her at the moment of truth?

Chapter Nineteen

It was 8:30 am, December 29, 2001. Normally an early riser, Marielle was still lying in Ghani's arms. She savored the feeling, knowing it would probably be the last time she felt his body close to hers. Or would it be? As the moment of truth grew closer and closer, Marielle's feelings for Ghani grew deeper and deeper, and her doubts about what she had to do grew stronger and stronger. She cuddled close to him and he awoke, turning over to lie upon her, his body enclosing her in what felt like a kiss of sorts for her whole body. He moved sensually and entered her, his kisses covering her mouth, her eyes and her neck. His lovemaking was ecstasy and she drowned her emotions in the glorious moment of it, savoring what she knew might be the last time they made love. Their passion for each other would never die, she thought, as he brought her to climax over and over again. When he had finally given her all that he could he held her lovingly in his arms.

"I love you more than life itself," he whispered, totally oblivious to the idea that his love for her might actually cost him his life.

"And I love you too," she answered as she turned her face into the pillows trying to hide the tears that started to fall. How could someone who was so loving to her be so hateful to others? He was not really a bad person. *Poor Ghani,* she thought. He too was a victim, a product of his environment, an environment that was poisoned by the brutality of a childhood bereft of mercy and human kindness.

If only he could have had the nurturing and unconditional love that she and Morty gave John Paul. He would have grown up to be a fine man, just like their son. She wondered if things would have been different had he known John Paul. Would watching their son grow up have helped Ghani overcome his hatred? Or would he have turned John Paul into the same monster that he grew into? It broke her heart to know that he was so unredeemable.

She remembered their early days together when she believed so much in him. Now there was nothing she could do to save him or change him, but that didn't mean she couldn't love him. *So many good qualities gone to waste,* she lamented. If only things had been different. If only she hadn't saved him from the Israelis. Perhaps they'd have just jailed him. After all it was in the US. He might have been rehabilitated. He was young then, too. She had been an unwitting enabler. *All this might never have happened,* she thought. It was a terrible burden to carry about, and it haunted her. As hard as it was to accept, it was at that moment she realized she had no choice but to carry out her mission. It was too late to change the past but it was not too late to change the future.

"Are you all right, darling?" he asked. "You seem so sad and far away."

"I'm a bit overwhelmed and I am sad there can't be peace on earth," she replied.

"Only Jihad will make your wish for peace possible," he said as he bent over and kissed her for what she knew was the very last time. She couldn't help the tears that flowed down her cheeks.

"Don't cry. These coming years will be the happiest time of our lives, I promise. You'll see," he said tenderly.

After he left she cried a little more, deep in thought, trying to muster the courage she needed to go through with what she came to do. She thought back to a very sad moment in her childhood. Her beloved dog, Trooper, a large, muscular German shepherd, bit a neighbor's child on the arm. The local police department felt Trooper might be a danger to the community because he tasted blood and that he should be destroyed. There was a hearing and it was decided that Trooper had to be put to sleep. Her mother gently broke the news to Marielle, and the police permitted them to take Trooper to the family veterinarian. Marielle loved Trooper but accepted his fate. Even as a child she could be counted on to do what had to be done.

Now, all these years later she envisioned that moment as if it were yesterday. Trooper followed her into the room, jumping up on the table. How he could jump and play! She smiled as she saw him in her mind's eye. He whined a little at the pinch of the injection, but was good and trusting as she petted his shoulder and kissed his furry forehead. She didn't cry or act differently. She didn't want Trooper to be afraid.

How similar this situation was, she thought. Ghani's hatred infected all these people so they became dangerous to society at large. *They can't be allowed to harm the world. What I must do is right. It is noble.*

Dear God Almighty, please understand why I must break one of your commandments. Please dear Jesus forgive me for not turning the other cheek. I am not that strong or good. I want revenge for John Paul and all the others. I want justice and a safe world free from this scourge called terrorism. When I am dead please allow my soul to be with the men who truly loved me: Morty, my dear husband and my friend, and John Paul, the heart of my heart, my baby boy. Ghani must meet his fate, and I must put a stop to his evil deeds. He must reap the wrath of the one true God.

As Marielle dressed herself she was in a state of high alert. She caught herself trembling with anticipation. Shortly after she finished dressing, Mahmoud came calling on her. Rima, he told her, was apprehended by Mullah Jazeera as she tried to leave the complex, but she poisoned herself with a cyanide tablet before she could be made to talk. Rima's suicide set off a panic among the mullahs, and word of her death reached Ghani who was making final preparations for Operation Palestinian Homeland in his war room.

His closest advisor, Hamda Qatar, saw this as an opportunity to once again question the credibility of Marielle. "Why did she come here? Rima was very close to her and the incident with the cameras highly suspicious, do you not think?" the little Palestinian man chided him.

Ghani shoved him and said, "I'll kill you if you ever say another disparaging word about her. Do you want to die?"

Hamda was shocked to see his leader so blinded by emotion for an infidel. There was no time to argue, and he didn't believe for a moment that a woman could hinder or compromise their master plan. He would find a way to deal with her later. Back in the private quarters Mahmoud told Marielle with a fearsome tone in his voice, "Madame, I believe she was hiding something and chose to die to keep the secret. I am frightened for you, Madame. I know you often spoke with her secretly. I worry that you have plotted something with her. I've suspected this for some days now, but I have told no one of my suspicions. I know you are a good woman. I'd never betray you because I owe you my life. I have faith in Allah but I have never truly believed in Jihad. I think you are trying to stop it so all the dying will end.

"Ghani expects you to join him in the great room in a few minutes for the ceremony before the martyrs leave. You are already running late but with Rima's suicide, I am not sure you should go at all.

There is no telling what will happen. I know Ali is your friend as well and they have already captured him and begun to torture him."

Marielle bent over, pretending to adjust the grandfather clock, ignoring Mahmoud's words. *Click, click, click, hard push.* How easily she set the bomb. There was no turning back now. She stood up straight now. Mahmoud grabbed her. "What have you done?" he demanded. "What did you do to that clock?"

Marielle half smiled. "I have done what I came here to do: to stop the senseless killing of innocents by misguided people. I am sorry, Mahmoud, you have been so kind to me and I truly appreciate it, but sadly we will all die here today. The bomb I have set cannot be stopped. It will detonate very soon. If anyone touches it, it will go off immediately."

Mahmoud understood the bravery of what Marielle did. He gave up his manhood to protect her, and now he realized what Allah's true purpose for him was all along. He *must* save her at all costs, even if it meant turning his back on his own people.

"Madame," he ordered, "get your riding clothes and chador. We are leaving the complex. We'll ride into the desert and escape the fires of Allah's wrath. Don't be afraid. I know a secret exit from these quarters and before we are missed we will be safe at the stables with Hope."

"Mahmoud, you don't understand. It is my fate to die with Ghani for saving his life so long ago. I don't want to go."

Mahmoud couldn't wait to argue with her anymore. *I am sorry for what I will do now,* he thought, *but I must try to save her.* With that, he hit Marielle with a sharp blow to the head, knocking her unconscious. He gathered her things and carried her through the secret doors to the tunnels leading to the underground rail system that went directly to the stables of the Mujahadim. Ghani showed him this escape route one time when he felt both he and Marielle might be in danger. So secret was this route that the Pakistani slaves who built it were killed upon its completion.

Mahmoud, truly a man with a mission, gently laid Marielle on the little rail car and prayed to Allah for their safety as they sped along in the dark tunnel with only a flashlight to lead the way.

Back in the great hall, Ghani waited for Marielle to join him for the blessing of the martyrs. She was now almost ten minutes late. He felt uncomfortable because being late was very unlike her, but he couldn't leave now because the mullahs had begun to pray.

Ghani stepped up to the podium but was not able to concentrate. *Where the hell is she?* he thought. He scanned the room, hoping to see her making her way to him.

The room was in a frenzy now at the sight of their leader, but he was distracted. The chanting grew louder, "Allah Akbar, Allah Akbar." He left the podium and pushed past some of the martyrs who had suitcase bombs handcuffed to their wrists the way Jewish jewelers often carry their most valuable items. This was a disguise that they hoped would go unnoticed in the hubbub of any city. They would be leaving on private jets after the ceremony for their destinations.

Ghani was oblivious to the confusion his hasty departure from the great hall created. Everyone was sure that their leader had lost his mind. Some were already suggesting that he be taken into custody and made to answer for his strange behavior. Unaware of all this, he ran back to their quarters, worrying that she had met with foul play. As he entered, he called her name frantically: "Marielle! Marielle!"

To his consternation he saw the secret door wide open. He stood frozen in disbelief, not knowing whether she had been abducted or had run away. Was Carlos right? Was she involved in a plot to destroy him? Had his love for her blinded him to what others clearly saw?

Then he noticed a soft hum coming from the grandfather clock and realized he'd been betrayed. Carlos and the others had been right. After looking closely at the clock he realized there was nothing he could do to disarm the bomb. As he realized all his plans were coming to an end, he slumped down in disbelief. *How could this be happening, how could I have been so blind?* he thought. He loved Marielle so much that he wound up sacrificing everything for her. Could it be that she had been pretending all along, that she came back to him not for love but for revenge? How could he have been so wrong about her feelings for him? Rage was now the only emotion he felt. "Marielle!" he screamed as he charged through the secret passageway door.

The Mujahadim riders had gone to the complex for the Day of Glory ceremonies, leaving the stables to their Pakistani slaves. Mahmoud was not going to take any chances, however, because the Pakistanis were known to be rabid supporters of Al Qaeda and Ghani Irabi. Mahmoud opened the heavy door at the end of the tunnel and broke through the wall, which led to the tack room.

One of the Pakistanis heard the noise and came to investigate. Mahmoud quickly overpowered him and slit his throat. He went into the aisle between the rows of stalls where two stablemen were watering the horses. They paid little attention to him. One by one he took their lives and dragged their bodies into the feed room where he threw several bags of grain over them. He went back to the secret entranceway where Marielle lay on the rail car. She was somewhat dazed and beginning to come to.

"Madame," he said as he dabbed at her bruised head with a cloth he soaked in cold water, "forgive me but I couldn't let you die. We must get away from here. Can you ride? Put on your jodhpurs. I've got them right here, as well as your chador. You must hurry. Madame, it's been more than fifteen minutes since you armed the bomb. How long do we have?" he said as he hurriedly began to saddle and bridle the horses.

"Another fifteen minutes at the most," she murmured. Her head throbbed and she was still a little dizzy.

When he finished tacking up the horses he opened all the stall doors to make sure the other noble steeds would escape. "Here. Get on Hope and ride like the wind. I'll be right beside you in case you feel faint. I know the desert. There is a Bedouin tribal area about twenty-five miles from here. We will be safe there."

He galloped alongside her. They let the horses have their heads, galloping forward at what is called a dead run. Two, three, five, six minutes passed as they raced to safety. Then suddenly a thunderous sound, followed by the ground shaking in such a way that both horses lost their footing and fell. Mahmoud was thrown clear of his mount but, like Marielle, was unhurt. The horses, though shaken and spooked, were fine.

Mahmoud saw it as a sign from Allah and fell to his knees to pray after he retrieved the terrified horses. Marielle, in shock but confident her job was finally over, said her own prayer of thanks to God.

She could hardly believe that she would see Caroline again; that she would know her grandchild. She was humbled by the fact that God saw fit to save her. She was relieved that all the radiation would be trapped underground. At the same time she was filled with an overwhelming sorrow, a sorrow she felt only once before in her life, when she learned of John Paul's fate. Now the other love of her life was gone. After all these years, Ghani had come back into her life and now once again he was gone. And this time the exit was final.

After riding for several hours, they rested at an oasis. The sun was setting so they decided to stay there for the night. Mahmoud had filled two saddlebags with grain for the horses. He and Marielle would make do with water until they reached the Bedouin camp.

They slept soundly under the star-filled desert sky. Mahmoud covered Marielle with both saddle blankets to protect her from the cold desert air.

They were completely unaware that Ghani had made it to the stables just before the bomb exploded. He saw blood on the floor leading to the tack room. He found one of the dead Pakistani slaves and realized that someone had to be helping Marielle. *It must be Mahmoud,* he thought. Some of the horses had not run away and he could hear them whinnying in the courtyard. Before he could run outside, the tremors from the explosion caused the stable walls to implode knocking him senseless.

Buried under the debris, he found it almost impossible to breathe. He began to think of his son buried beneath the World Trade Center. He wondered if his son had suffered and now he knew what it felt like to be trapped and covered in debris gasping for air, unable to see. He wondered if anyone was alive back at the complex. In a panic, he began to dig himself out with one arm. His other arm was numb or maybe broken. It took him about an hour to dig himself out.

He found some bandages and a rope and fashioned a makeshift sling for his right arm. He caught one of the few remaining horses and took off after Marielle.

Crazed by her betrayal, he could only think of tracking her down and confronting her for what she did. Ghani, too, knew of the Bedouin camp and surmised they'd head there for help.

When he came upon them both asleep, horses tethered nearby, he quietly dismounted and tied his mount with theirs.

Moving like a cat toward her with the night so brightly lit by the multitude of stars, he could see her beautiful face framed in moonlight.

He planned to shoot them both on sight but now he wasn't sure what to do. There were too many questions in his mind. He needed answers. How could he have been so blind? How could he have trusted her so completely? All his life he had been so very cautious about everyone and now this. Carlos could see it. So could the others. Why couldn't he? Why did Allah allow his soldier to be so blinded by love? Lost in thought, he didn't know how long he sat there just watching her. Suddenly Mahmoud awoke and, seeing Ghani with a gun, jumped up and lunged at him, partly to shield Marielle and partly to disarm him.

Ghani was a powerful man, however, and he knocked Mahmoud cold with his first blow to his head.

Hearing the commotion Marielle awoke and was on her feet in a second. She was shocked to see that Ghani was still alive. She had been sure she would never see him again and now here he was. She was overcome with both fear and a strange sort of relief. Reacting instinctively with the skills she learned from her CIA training she kicked the gun out of Ghani's hand. She prepared to fight for her life. However, she was no match for Ghani and he quickly subdued her. He dragged her with him as he retrieved his gun.

"Marielle," he said shaking her, "Why did you betray me? I loved you more than anything in this world and this is how you repay me? I chose you over my own people, over my brother Carlos. I gave you everything you asked for and in return you have destroyed everything I worked for, you have destroyed me. Why? Was it revenge for the death of our son? Did the CIA send you here? You must tell me. You must at least give me that. And most of all I must know if your love was a lie. Was it all a game? Did you ever really love me as I have really loved you?" His eyes were filled with tears, and they began to run down his cheeks.

With the realization she had no chance against this man, Marielle was ready to die. She wasn't afraid.

"Ghani," she said, as the tears began to fall from her eyes. "I have and do love you more than anything else in this world. I love you more than life itself. But you've become so evil, so completely without mercy in your fanaticism that someone had to try to stop you. Someone had to stop you from causing any further harm to the people of the world. I chose to deliver that justice to you for John Paul and all the other innocents whose lives you have taken in the name of your misguided Jihad. I chose to deliver that justice to protect all the innocent people who you would otherwise hurt in the future. Because I love you so much this was the hardest decision I've ever had to make. But you had to be stopped. I intended to die with you, by your side. If it had been my choice I would have been standing with you in the great hall when the bomb went off. We would have perished together. For some reason God saw fit to use Mahmoud to bring us both here instead."

Ghani listened intently to each of Marielle's words. He was filled with conflicting emotions. On the one hand he had devoted his entire life to trying to help his people. While his methods may have been radical, it was the world's neglect which made those methods necessary. It was the ignorant world which ignored the plight of his people. They needed to pay for this, it was Allah's will. He was just doing what had to be done. And now this woman had taken away his ultimate victory. How could he not avenge her actions? How could he let her live?

On the other hand he loved this woman. The best time in his life had been the short time he spent with her. She made him feel things he never felt before, feelings of fulfillment and love. He knew her intentions were good. He was convinced she really loved him. How could he possibly take a life so precious to him? He had already unintentionally killed their son. Could he kill her too?

The struggle going on in his mind lasted only a few moments but felt like forever to him. He had failed his people, he had failed his son, would he now fail the love of his life? He was confused. He prayed that Allah would guide his actions. Suddenly, his mind was at peace.

"Oh Marielle, my poor dear Marielle. Why didn't you tell me these things when I asked? I'd have protected you. You have no need to fear me. I could never really harm you. I love you too much. Even after all you've done, I love you. I thought I could kill you but in truth I cannot. I am sorry for John Paul and all the sons and daughters and mothers and fathers. And most of all I am sorry that I forced you to do what you have done."

He began to cry, "You are right about everything. I admire the courage it must have taken for you to come here and try to stop me. To destroy my plans Allah had to be with you, on your side. It is all so clear now. I now understand Allah's will and why I came to love you so. Why he allowed me to be so blinded by my love for you. So Allah could stop me and those like me. I now understand why Allah has brought us both here at this moment. I now know what I must do."

He raised the gun. *I will try to be brave,* Marielle thought as she braced herself for the bullet.

"Your love for me has been the best thing in my life. And now, my final act of love for you. Goodbye, my love," he said turning the gun on himself and pulling the trigger.

He let go of her as his body fell backwards to the ground. His blood was everywhere. At once she was by his side cradling his head.

"Oh Ghani, you never had a chance. Your childhood and the horror of it sealed your fate."

"Don't hate me, Marielle," he gasped as blood trickled from his lips. "Please, don't hate me. Remember me for the good we had together, for my love of you."

"My darling, how could I hate you? I never hated you. I have loved you from the first moment you looked in my eyes those many years ago. And I love you now. I only hated the things you did. I know you were a victim, too."

"Hold me, Marielle, hold me one last time," he moaned barely audible. "What is that light? It's so bright. I can't see you anymore."

"It's Allah, Ghani," she said tenderly. "He's come to take you to Paradise. Finally you can be at peace."

"I am forgiven," he said, his voice trailing off as she felt his soul leave his body. She sobbed as she laid his head down gently on the sand.

"My lion of the desert, may Allah let you rest in peace."

After a few moments Marielle went to attend to Mahmoud. He had a large abrasion on his forehead from where Ghani had hit him. He was starting to come to.

"Madame, Madame. I am so glad you are alive. I am sorry. I tried to protect you. What has happened?"

"Ghani took his own life. Can you get up and help put his body on his horse. I want him to have a proper burial here in the desert where he belongs. Do you think the Bedouins will help us?"

"We will bury him here as they did in days of old. He would want the site of his grave kept secret. I will help you with this final task you must perform."

"I loved him, Mahmoud," she said. "But someone had to end the madness."

"I know Madame," he said. "Allah chose you."

As soon as the sun rose, they saddled up and were on their way again toward the camp.

Meanwhile in Langley, Red Connors and the director were going over the satellite photographs of the explosion and measuring the radiation emanating from the area of the compound.

"The explosion was eight or ten times greater than the load in our device," Red remarked. "We must have destroyed all the missing Russian suitcase bombs. The little lady hit the nail right on the head," he said proudly.

The director got a call and was stunned. "What!—She's alive? You've picked up satellite photos showing two people riding away from the area before the explosion? A woman and a man? Well I'll be damned. Red Connors, you trained a superwoman."

"That's what it's all about, Sir. We try," Red answered smugly.

"They're sending a team to extract her even as we speak," the director added. "She'll be able to shed some light on just what happened over there. What a woman she's turned out to be."

As Mahmoud and Marielle reached the Bedouin camp, they heard the hum of engines in the distance. As they came closer, they saw the noise came from a couple of military vehicles, a truck and a car. The lead car bore two American flags on either side of its radiator. A man got out and came toward them.

"Hello. I'm James Goodwin, the US ambassador to Yemen. I'm here to take you home, Mrs. Bennett. You are one brave woman. You *are* Marielle Bennett, aren't you?"

"Yes I am," said a weary Marielle, overjoyed to see this man. She managed to dismount and shake his hand. "This is Mahmoud el Said. He saved my life. I'm so happy and relieved to see you, but I'd like you to know that I'm not leaving without Mahmoud or my horse, Hope, and the black beauty over there, for that matter."

The ambassador laughed. "That's what the truck is for, ma'am. I've already been briefed that you'd most likely want to bring the horse. What the hell, we have room for both. And Mr. Said, well it sounds like you just saved the right person, and have won a free trip to the good old U. S. of A."

Epilogue—Two Years Later

THE WEATHER WAS PERFECT THAT EARLY SPRING DAY. The sea splashed on the shore while Marielle walked by herself, watching the sunrise trumpeting a new day. It was the same beach where long ago she and Ghani stole away for a holiday, the beach where John Paul was conceived. She was flooded with memories, happy and bittersweet.

She wanted closure, but it eluded her. She still wore the yellow diamond ring, its sparkle blinding as it flashed in the sunlight. She walked into the water waist deep and began to swim toward the rising sun. She slipped the ring from her finger and let it go. "Goodbye, my love," she whispered.

She was quickly interrupted as she heard Mahmoud calling, "Madame, Madame, breakfast is ready." She returned to the beach and ran up to the veranda, where he held a towel for her.

"Hurry, Madame. Caroline and little John Paul will be down soon." She went into the big, open kitchen and sat down.

"Grammy, Grammy," she heard a tiny voice say. "Me want to swimming." Her precious little grandson climbed into her lap and begged to go to the water.

"We have to eat breakfast first, my little one," she told the impatient little boy. Caroline came in, saw John Paul and his Grammy and realized she at last found the relationship with her mother she longed for. She thought of her brother and how tickled he would have been with his namesake. Little John Paul could think of only one thing; to go play in the water.

"Eat your breakfast, boy," Mahmoud said, "then I'll take you for a swim."

Caroline walked over and put her hand on her mother's shoulder. "We're lucky, you know," she said. "In all this pain we've found the most important thing of all. Mummy, we've found each other."